THE TEACHER'S FUNERAL

THE TEACHER'S FUNERAL
A Comedy in Three Parts

RICHARD PECK

SCHOLASTIC INC.
New York Toronto London Auckland Sydney
Mexico City New Delhi Hong Kong Buenos Aires

ISBN 0-439-80266-0

Published by Scholastic Inc., 557 Broadway, New York, NY 10012, by arrangement with Dial Books for Young Readers, a member of Penguin Group (USA) Inc.

12 11 10 9 8 7 6 5 4 3 2   5 6 7 8 9 10/0

Printed in the U.S.A.   23

First Scholastic printing, September 2005

Designed by Lily Malcom

Text set in Stempel Garamond

Table of Contents

THE TEACHER'S FUNERAL

Part I

Kissing Summer Good-Bye

☆ ☆ ☆

Chapter One

August

If your teacher has to die, August isn't a bad time of year for it. You know August. The corn is earring. The tomatoes are ripening on the vine. The clover's in full bloom. There's a little less evening now, and that's a warning. You want to live every day twice over because you'll be back in the jailhouse of school before the end of the month.

Then our teacher, Miss Myrt Arbuckle, hauled off and died. It was like a miracle, though she must have been forty. You should have seen my kid brother's face. It looked like Lloyd was hearing the music of the spheres. Being ten that summer, he was even more willing to believe in miracles than I was.

You couldn't deny Miss Myrt Arbuckle was past her prime. She was hard of hearing in one ear, no doubt deafened by her own screaming. And she couldn't whup us like she wanted to. She was a southpaw for whupping, and she had arthritis in that elbow, so while she could still whup, it didn't make much of an impression.

Back in the spring when she called up Lester Kriegbaum for some infraction, nothing serious, he brought a book to the front of the room and read it over her knee while she larruped away at his far end.

So when you get right down to it, if you can't hear and you can't whup, you're better off dead than teaching. That's how I looked at it.

There was always talk about shutting down Hominy Ridge School anyhow. Now that me and Lloyd saw its end might be nigh, hope broke over us. It was surely too late to find another teacher who'd teach in a place like that.

Hominy Ridge was nothing but an out-of-date, unimproved, one-room country schoolhouse in the backwoodsiest corner of Indiana. They admitted it didn't pay to keep it for just us straggle of kids who went there.

Dad was on the school board. Me and Lloyd hoped to encourage him to close down the school and drive all formal education out of this part of Parke County. For one thing, I'd been fifteen since winter and still hadn't passed the eighth-grade graduation exam.

Besides, I had me a dream, and school only stood in my way.

"Russell, will they have a funeral for Miss Myrt?" Lloyd looked up at me, wondering.

"Of course they'll have a funeral for her," I said. "Did you think they'd just feed her to the hogs?"

But I know how Lloyd thought. Regular people have funerals, but Miss Myrt was a teacher. As for a funeral, it was hot weather and the crops were in the ground and the roads were dry and the fair was over. "What else do people have to do?" I said. "They'll turn out for Miss Myrt."

"They better," Lloyd said darkly. "She's liable to set up in her coffin and take roll."

Chapter Two

The Best Boys in the World

How we learned that Miss Myrt Arbuckle had turned up her toes gets ahead of the story. This news didn't reach us till almost midnight, and then under dramatic circumstances.

But it had been a red-letter day anyhow, the main day of the year for me, better than the 4th of July. It was the day the J. I. Case Company of Racine, Wisconsin, sent their special train down through Indiana. We'd watched for the flyers announcing it all summer. My heart was in my mouth that Dad wouldn't let us go.

The Case Special came through every August with flatcars of the latest in steam engines and threshing machines. It was better than a circus. Every man and boy from twenty miles around converged on Montezuma to see the Case Special. I walked the floor all night for fear Dad would keep us in the field. I hadn't figured out he wouldn't have missed the Case Special himself.

Me and Lloyd were up ahead of the chickens. We worked a seven-day week anyway, even in this quiet season. As Dad said, the only man who got his work done by Friday was Robinson Crusoe. And we were a corn, wheat, hay, and hogs farm in a never-ending round of chores, plus the milking. Today me and Lloyd were a pair of whirlwinds—two tornados back and forth to the barn a dozen times before breakfast. And it was already hot enough to fry your brains through your hat.

Then we pulled cockleburs out of the corn into the heat of the day. Cockleburs have two seeds that mature at different times, so you have to kill them twice. All the while, one cricket after another walked in under our hickory shirts on bobwire legs and made life a misery. Still, we worked ahead of Dad all morning, the best boys in the world, and Dad never let on that he knew why.

You talk about hot. They don't make Augusts like that anymore. An old horsethief from just over in Putnam County died and went down to Hades. And he sent back for a blanket. That's the kind of heat we were used to. At long last we heard the dinner bell sound from the house.

When we came to the end of the row, we saw Dad up in the lot, bent over the horse trough. He wasn't just washing a little bit for the dinner table. He was washing his whole top half. That meant he was fixing to go to town. Lloyd was ready to rip out a whoop, but I put a lid on him. We weren't there yet.

I thought if we had to take the time to sit down to dinner, we'd be too late to see the Case Special come in. But the hand that rang the dinner bell was our sister Tansy's. And if she cooked, you sat and ate it.

Tansy was named for a wildflower, which suited her because she was just as countrified and rawboned as me and Lloyd, almost. She was our big sister—great big, and she loomed over our lives.

"Let's see those hands." Tansy gave the back of my head a painful thump. There was no arthritis in her elbows. She had a pancake turner in her other hand, so I showed her my palms.

"Well, I see where you've been," she remarked, and she didn't mean the trough. She passed along to Lloyd. "You should have left more of the field where it was," said she after a look at his paws.

"We washed," Lloyd whined. I had the sense to keep quiet. "We washed in the trough, same as Dad."

Dad obliged by turning up his palms, but Tansy thought Lloyd deserved the same thump she'd given me. She was fair that way. "Ow!" Lloyd exclaimed.

"Do you have such a thing as a lump of soap down at the trough?" Tansy inquired.

"No," said Lloyd, who never learned. "It'd gag the horses. They'd foam at the mouth."

Dad gazed out the door and down the corn rows, trying not to smile.

"Now I see your neck and ears," Tansy told Lloyd, "I'm gagging myself."

"Let 'em be so they can eat," Aunt Maud called out from the stove. I was wolfing it down already, crazy to head for town. But we had a good big dinner to get through first: chicken-fried steak, boiled potatoes and cream gravy, a platter of dead-ripe, deep red beefsteak tomatoes, and a pyramid of pickled peaches in the cut-glass dish. We were being force-fed last year's pickled peaches to make way for this year's.

Aunt Maud pulled down the oven door and drew out a sheet of her drop biscuits. Dad's thorny hand covered his eyes. Aunt Maud was the worst baker in the United States. You couldn't use her dough balls for bait.

She was no better a cook. We lived for summer because Tansy was home to do most of the cooking for us. In the fall she went back to board in town, to go to the high school. Why Tansy needed to go to high school was another of life's mysteries to me.

"Pie's pretty nearly baked!" she declared. "Who wants a slab?" But by then Lloyd was halfway to the back door, and Dad right on his heels.

We hitched up Siren and Stentor to the spring wagon

and off we went along the boiling roads. Somehow we made it to town with minutes to spare. It beat me why Tansy and Aunt Maud didn't want to go.

"Gawk at a bunch of implements in the Montezuma railroad yard with all those cinders underfoot?" Tansy said. "I thank you, no."

It occurred to me even that early in life that there's not much romance in a woman's soul. The very names of the big steam threshers turned my heart over: the Geiser Peerless, the Minnesota Little Giant, the Avery Yellow Fellow, the Pitts Challenger, the Frick Eclipse.

Finally our wagon was in a row with others, down the hill into town. This was the biggest crowd we saw from one year to the next. An acre of wagons drew up by the depot. Two hundred straw hats bobbed against the punishing sun, and not a bonnet among us.

This is how I pictured Indianapolis, this crush of humankind with nary a familiar face. I looked for my best friend, Charlie Parr, but didn't see him. Of course he could have been an arm's length away, and I wouldn't know. You could scarcely draw breath, and not every farmer had stopped by the trough on the way here.

Then in the farthest distance we heard a trill. It was the steam calliope on the Case Special, flinging a tune to the four winds. The sound of music coming down the tracks made every hair on my head stand up. Though he was too big to hold my hand, Lloyd had me in a grip. It was the Case Special.

Smoke billowed, and the whistle screamed as the train roared in. The shrieking brakes set, and live steam singed our bare feet. On the car past the calliope a Farmer's Friend wind stacker blew out circulars and handbills instead of chaff. Paper and then tin buttons with the Case eagle on them rained over us.

Now we were waiting for Uncle Sam and the Gold Dust Twins because we wanted every year to be just like last year. As the calliope swung into "Marching Through Georgia," Uncle Sam unfolded himself out of the caboose. He stood over us, twelve feet tall in spangled top hat and stilts.

But we were lost to him. The Gold Dust Twins couldn't hold us either, even when they bucked-and-winged into "Under the Bamboo Tree" and threw soapy scouring pads for our womenfolk. A cloud passed, and the full glare of the sun fell on this year's 1904 models of the Case Agitator threshing machine.

They were steel.

Threshing machines had been wooden-sided from the beginning. But these monsters were sheet steel. We were blinded by their sheen. The twentieth century had found us at last, even here. We didn't know how to look at something so new. A lump formed in my throat.

Now Uncle Sam was calling somebody up out of the mob. An Agitator was fired up and steaming. Somebody was wanted to feed lumber into the rig to prove how rugged these new steel models were. If the Agitator could do this to hardwood, think what it could do to your wheat crop.

The face Uncle Sam lit upon was Charlie Parr's. He was older than me, though he hadn't passed the eighth-grade graduation examination either. He swung up on the flatcar and commenced feeding stove lengths into the Agitator. The sawdust blew a dry cloudburst over us.

My mind was miles away by then, up in the Dakotas. I caught a glimpse of me up there for the wheat harvest. I was working one of these all-steel Case Agitators across the thousand-mile fields, under endless sky. I saw me doing a man's work on a crew of men who'd logged all winter. I felt the chaff in my hair.

All I wanted was to be on a threshing crew, to be in the stubble fields on crisp mornings like the dawn of creation. When I'd get back after the harvest I couldn't tell you. How cold it got up there I didn't know. But that was my dream, and school stood between me and it.

Lloyd tightened his grip on me. He knew I was fixing to go, that in my heart I was already gone.

Chapter Three

Me and Lloyd and Charlie Parr

"All right, Gold Dust Twins." Tansy put out her hand. "Let's have those soap pads." We handed them over, having no use for them ourselves.

Behind her on the kitchen table two parcels were tied up in napkins: cold fried chicken, a roasting ear, a jar each of pickled peaches for sure, and I don't know what all. "I made the shortened biscuits myself," Tansy said, speaking low because Aunt Maud was somewhere about the place.

This was the night me and Lloyd always went to the crick and camped out. It was a sacred part of our year. After the Case Special came through, we always spent that night at the crick, and hung on till morning, no matter what. It was how we kissed the summer goodbye before the darkness of learning fell about us.

And we felt the shades of eternal night falling fast because at this point, remember, we supposed Miss Myrt Arbuckle was alive and kicking and drawing up her lessons for another nightmare year.

A trip to town tired Dad more than a full day in the field, one more thing about being grown up I didn't understand. He sent us off to the crick on our own. He expected me to look out for Lloyd, and I did, though in my own particular way.

It was a fishing trip, but Tansy had little faith in us as fishermen. She packed us more than we could eat if we got lost for a week and never found the crick. I'll give her credit, though: She made up a can of dough balls for our bait.

We left Stentor at home to graze and hitched Siren to the spring wagon. She wasn't as crazy as we were for another trip this soon, so we let her see us throw handfuls of alfalfa and oats and horse weeds into the wagon bed, and she was resigned. There was no getting away without J.W., of course.

He capered out from under the porch where he lived in hot weather, and ran circles around us, dropping down to slide his hind end in the weeds. He was Dad's dog. Dad had trained him to run coons, but he couldn't be broke from running rabbits instead, and couldn't grasp the difference. His initials stood for "Just Worthless." After two tries, he was up in the wagon, among the oats, whimpering with joy and confusion and looking everywhere for his tail.

At last we were off down the road with the setting sun casting long shadows before us. The dogs from every farm we went by raced out to see us past, and J.W., lolling over the wagon side, told them all about it.

Chickens having their dust baths in the road dived for the ditch, and Siren kicked up her heels a little bit along the straightaway. There aren't a lot of perfect moments in life. This was one.

We went past the Leadill place. Then as we were coming past the Parrs', Lloyd said, "How come Charlie's not going with us?"

Charlie always went. It was part of our regular plan. But I told Lloyd Charlie thought he was getting too old for doings like this. Lloyd wondered why anybody thought he was too old to go to the crick.

It was the Little Shady which flowed into the Wabash which flowed into the Ohio and so forth. It was slow and mostly shallow. We camped by a grove a few rods from the road. We weren't two miles from home, but the crick was somewhere else. How far off the Dakotas were I didn't know.

There was a circle of stones from years past for our fire. Once we unhitched Siren and tied her up, we made a manger for her in the bole of the tree. J.W. went to work clearing the vicinity of rabbits while me and Lloyd began to string our trotlines.

That's how we fished. Most of the Little Shady was shallow enough to wade. Lloyd plunged in first with a line to attach to something on the other bank. He carried the can of dough balls on a piece of twine around his neck. There were hooks spaced along the trotline, and we hung a dough ball on each. Then through the night we could pull on the line from the bank to feel if there was a fish on it. When there was, we'd wade out, take it off the hook, and bait that hook again. We ran six or eight lines across the crick.

Living in hope, we brought a skillet and a pat of lard. But we were apt to catch sunfish and cat too small to keep. Once in a while we'd get a five-pounder or bigger. Once in a great while. Charlie Parr scorned our kind of fishing. He liked what he called "loggin'." He'd stalk out into the deepest part of the channel to where logs were sunk. Then he'd reach down under the log and grab a fish in his big bare hands. Of course he ran the risk that it was something else. Charlie's arms were pitted with the scars of snapping turtles, which he wore with pride.

We were drenched from horsing around in the crick and stepping in holes we couldn't see. It was still pretty nearly as hot as midday. Steam rose off the water and Siren. Now here came a bloodred moon on the rise through the sycamores while purple light still faded in the west.

We built up the fire and, naturally starved, thought we'd try one piece each of Tansy's fried chicken. Wanting his share, J.W. hunkered forward through the weeds. We sat there around a fire that began to feel good. Lloyd picked burs out of J.W.'s matted pelt. A couple of old screech owls swooped up a hedgerow, looking for mice. Me and Lloyd speculated about using pickled peaches for bait. A star or two began to show. It would have been another of life's perfect moments except for the mosquitoes and chiggers and whatever was crawling off J.W. and onto us.

You can hear farther in the dark. Now the night life of the river came forth to feed on one another. Above us we heard the crunch of bugs in beaks. Fish flopped. A noisy frog gave itself away and screamed as something bigger swallowed it.

I waited for just the right moment: this one.

Then I said to Lloyd, "It's a durn good thing we got past the graveyard in daylight." The old Balm of Gilead cemetery was along Quagmire Road, about halfway between here and home.

A breeze came up and ruffled our flesh. Lloyd kept picking things off J.W. He wouldn't rise to my bait.

I pressed on. "Because of Old Man Lichtenberger."

Still picking, Lloyd said at last, "What about him?"

"Well, they planted him last Wednesday, didn't they?" It hadn't been much of a funeral. Nobody we knew went.

"So what?" Lloyd wouldn't meet my eye, though I was staring a hole in him.

"You know how these medical students come out and work the territory, after dark."

"Why?" reluctant Lloyd said, though he knew. He

knew. The hook wasn't in his mouth, but the dough ball was.

"They got to have cadavers to cut up for their medical studies," I explained. "There's never enough cadavers to go around. How you going to know about people's insides if you don't own a set yourself? And a cadaver's expensive when you can get one on the open market. You try buying a dead body. Them medical students work the whole state of Indiana for free cadavers they can dig up theirselves."

"Naw," Lloyd said.

"After dark," I said.

Lloyd pulled on his little pointed chin. He tried to look older and wiser. The fire crackled between us. He wouldn't look at me, though he felt my eyes upon him, and darkness at his back.

"You trying to spook me, Russell?" he inquired.

"I'm just saying," I said.

"Anyhow, Old Man Lichtenberger would be pretty ripe by now," Lloyd said hopefully. "Ripe and runny. It's been a hot spell here lately."

"Well, it won't matter in his case, will it?" I said, ready for this.

"Won't it?"

J.W. sighed in Lloyd's lap.

"He was an old soak," I said. "Dad himself said Old Man Lichtenberger hadn't been sober since Garfield was President."

"So what?" Lloyd said faintly.

"That's the kind of cadaver the medical students look for, one that's already preserved in alcohol—a drunkard's corpse."

Silence, while the words *drunkard's corpse* sank into Lloyd. Then he said, "He'd smell bad, though, wouldn't he?" Lloyd was beginning to see the picture—the open grave steaming by lantern light.

"Real bad," I said. "But they're naturally desperate, these medical students. It'd be more than your life was worth if you come across them opening a grave." I was half spooked myself by now. "And they've got to be real careful lifting a cadaver out of a coffin, to keep it from coming apart."

Lloyd swallowed.

Night wind rose in the rustling corn with a rattlesnake sound. "The medical students will hit pay dirt with Old Man Lichtenberger," I said, summing up. "So to speak. I hear he was buried with a full bottle of brush whiskey to keep him from getting thirsty and restless."

"I don't think so," Lloyd said, uncertain. "They wouldn't do that. No preacher would put up with it."

"I'm just saying what the grown-ups say when kids aren't around." Meaning Lloyd was a kid and I wasn't. He was on the hook now, and I didn't know how long I could keep him there. Silence lingered too long. I looked into the grove and saw nothing. The fire began to burn down. I seemed to nod off.

Then I jerked alert. Some sound strangulated out of my throat. Lloyd was surprised into looking right at me. He saw one of my hands clapped over my mouth and my eyes starting out of my head. My other hand pointed past Lloyd to the dark grove behind him.

At this selfsame moment J.W. came awake and backed out of Lloyd's lap, which was perfect. Lloyd whirled around, following my pointing finger. The grove was darker than a crow's insides now. But just at the farthest finger of firelight, between two sycamores, something was standing.

It looked taller than a man, a terrible, tattered figure, faceless in the leafy shadow. In its big, knobby, earth-blackened hand it held . . . a whiskey bottle.

"Ohhh, leave me be," it moaned, gravely, like wind weeping in treetops. "Don't defile my body."

Lloyd dropped backward off his log.

Instead of lunging forward to protect us, J.W. backed into the weeds, growling and whining.

Lloyd was on his feet now. His breath came in sobs. He staggered sideways on his spindly legs, tripped over his own foot, and fell full-length into the crick. The water wasn't crotch-deep on a dwarf at that point. But Lloyd went right under.

Charlie Parr walked out of the grove and up to the fire. "Have you et all Tansy's chicken?" he asked, flipping the empty whiskey bottle into the weeds. J.W. yelped.

Charlie hadn't emptied the bottle himself. He could be a handful, but even he wouldn't take up hard liquor. His dad was the Methodist preacher. Us Culvers were Methodists too. It meant you could do pretty much as you pleased as long as you didn't drink liquor or dance. Especially dance. Us Methodists said dancing was nothing but hugging to music.

Lloyd thrashed in the black water and finally found his feet. He'd gone in face-first, which hid his tears. "You dirty rat, Russell," he hollered, spitting like a cat.

He stood in the crick, sopping and streaming. "You knowed that was Charlie. Him and you cooked this up."

"Did I say it right?" Charlie asked me, beginning to rifle through Tansy's eats.

Lloyd stalked out of the crick and teetered on the bank. He was shaking with rage and wetness. He wouldn't come near us, but he wanted by the fire. He was on the horns of a dilemma.

"You've scared off every fish between here and the Wabash River at Vincennes," I remarked.

"Shut up, Russell," Lloyd spat. "Just shut—"

"Oh, I don't know," Charlie said. "You might could have something on the hook already." He'd been hunkered before the fire and our food supply. Now he stood up, way up. He was about six foot three. He wandered over to the bank and began to pull on our trotlines. "Hey, you got somethin' here."

Lloyd was interested in spite of himself as Charlie strolled into the crick, following a line. We could use a mess of fish with Charlie around. He could eat you out of house and home, and he was too big to argue with. His thick fist followed the line till he came to a heavy hook. He grabbed there and heaved up.

My heart skipped a beat. Breaking the surface of the water was a writhing snake. It was thicker than Charlie's wrist and an easy four foot long. I saw fangs and the pitiless gleam of an eye. The sickening white of its twisting belly flashed in the firelight. All I could think of was water moccasin. Now it was off the hook, whipping in the air like a wrangler's rope.

"Sweet—" Charlie exclaimed, and his feet shot out from under him. He went down in the crick, full-length, with another almighty splat. Where the snake went you couldn't see, and Charlie didn't linger to find out. He was out of that crick like he could walk on water. I'd never seen that boy move so fast, not even on Hallowe'en night.

When he got to the bank, he was still traveling, and breathing real hard when he got to the fire. "You get the next one," he gasped.

Then we were all sitting around the fire. We'd built it up with brush and pine knots to dry out these two, and Charlie's dunking seemed some solace to Lloyd.

Charlie recovered pretty quick, because he said, "Them biscuits Tansy's or your aunt Maud's?"

"Aunt Maud's," I said, and Lloyd agreed, to keep Charlie from picking us clean. The chicken was already gone.

It was dead of night now with a ring around the moon. J.W. came back from his patrol, limping with a bur between his toes, and crept into Lloyd's damp lap.

You could hear any distance now, even above the whine of the katydids. Way off somewhere a dog howled at the moon, and other dogs picked up his wolfish cry. Even J.W.'s ears pricked, though he never moved.

"That howling only means but one thing," Charlie remarked, "and you know what."

"What?" Lloyd said.

"Dogs always know when somebody's died."

"No, sir, you're not getting me again, Charlie. You either, Russell," Lloyd piped in a thin and wobbling voice, "you dirty—"

"I ain't talking about gettin' anybody," Charlie said. "Somebody did die tonight. That's why we—I was late. Everybody's telling everybody else. You're the only two who don't know nothin' about it."

He had me about half interested. It wasn't like Charlie to pull something on his own. He didn't have that much imagination. "How'd you find out?" I asked, to see what he'd say. Charlie didn't think quick enough to lie.

"Party line," he said.

It was true that the Parrs subscribed to the telephone. We Culvers did too. "Who died?" I inquired.

"Take a guess," Charlie said. "Go ahead."

"Somebody we know?"

"You can believe that."

"Somebody old or young?"

"Old," Charlie said, "as the hills."

Lloyd was looking back and forth between us, clutching J.W. He was on the hook again, and I was getting there.

"Old as Old Man Lichtenberger?"

"Nobody's that old," Charlie said.

"Man or woman?"

"That'd be tellin' too much."

"Somebody we like?"

"Not hardly," Charlie said.

"Somebody who's been feeling poorly late?" I was wracking my brains.

Charlie shrugged his big shoulders. "She must of felt pretty poorly tonight. She died."

"So it's a woman!"

"More or less," Charlie said.

The truth burst over me. "You don't mean Miss Myrt Arbuckle!"

"You got her," Charlie said. "She's dead as mutton."

"Charlie, you lying—"

"No, Russell, believe me or believe me not. Miss Myrt kicked the bucket right about supper time."

"Prove how you know." I narrowed my eyes.

"Well, she rooms and boards with Miz Cooper, and when Miz Cooper rung the doctor, everybody picked up. My ma did. You can bet your aunt Maud did."

That was the beauty of the old party line telephone. A call for one was a call for all. When somebody rang for the doctor—two long rings and a short one—everybody picked up.

"When Miss Myrt didn't come to supper, Miz Cooper went to her room. The old hen was stretched out on the bed, deader than a doornail. Doc Wilkinson told Miz Cooper to put pennies on Miss Myrt's eyes to keep them closed till he could get there. And he said to tie up her jaw with a rag to keep it from sagging. So she's shut up at last."

Lloyd's eyes were wide and staring. His jaw hung open.

I was almost speechless with amazement, but not quite. "What killed her?"

"You got me," Charlie said. "All I know for sure is she's cut her last switch."

Many's the time she'd striped Charlie Parr's other end, back before the arthritis got in her elbow. Though he was a preacher's son, it was at school where he learned to turn the other cheek. Charlie still walked with a slight limp.

As I say, it was like a miracle, if you could believe it. Miss Myrt dying practically on the eve of school starting up. In August.

"She'll be a restless spirit," Charlie observed. "She'll be a soul in torment, carried off just when she was fixing to lock us up in that schoolhouse for another year."

I hadn't thought of it like that. And I didn't have time to wonder how Charlie did. Somehow, it didn't sound much like Charlie.

Lloyd sat studying the fire, wanting with his whole heart to believe. Him and Charlie sat with their backs to the grove, so I was the one to see Siren. She slept on her feet, and she'd dozed through everything so far. Now she nickered and pulled back on her rope. Her tail whipped around. The firelight caught one of her eyes rolling back with fear.

That was all the warning in the world I got. Siren nickered again, and I seemed to hear the answering nicker of another horse, far off. The mist in the grove was blue now, and a patch of the darkness changed. The underbrush crackled, as if from a footfall. Something was moving in the timber.

A hand pushed back a low-hanging limb. I saw her then, just a darkness against deeper dark. I saw the shawl over her head. Now the firelight found her. She stopped, keeping this distance from the living. More shadows puddled at her feet.

I could see nothing but her eyes, and I knew them from somewhere. Beneath the shadowing shawl her head was tied up with a rag—to keep her dead jaw from dropping in one final gape.

She stood there until her glinting eyes found mine. My heart had stopped by then, so I could have heard every word she spoke. She was silent as eternity, quieter than snow. One of her draped arms began to come up, slow because she had arthritis in that elbow. She seemed about to point at me, which would naturally have finished me off right there. Instead, she held up something: an untidy bundle of switches. She'd gathered them in the grove, for the grave.

My heart gave a single thump, and I was ready to travel, faster than Charlie at his top speed. I was on my feet, grunting like a bullbat. What Lloyd and Charlie were doing I didn't know. I meant to save myself. At that very moment, a live coal rolled out of the fire. In my first fleeing step, I trod my bare foot right on that red-hot coal. The soles of our feet were tough as whang-leather by this time of year, but that was a sizable coal.

"Eyeow!" I screamed in fear and pain. This was happening directly in front of Charlie. When I kicked up my foot, he saw that the live coal was still stuck to the sole of it. With unusual presence of mind, Charlie leaped to his feet and grabbed me up like a sack of flour. The next thing I knew, I was in the crick. Charlie'd thrown me right in the middle of it. I was sucking water on the slimy bottom. My foot was still burning but not alight. I couldn't think. I was burning up and drowning, and I'd just seen a ghost. Took me forever to distinguish up from down and break the surface of the water.

The first thing I saw was my sister, Tansy, with a shawl thrown back over her shoulders. She stood in the dancing firelight, unwinding the rag that had held her jaw closed. Charlie and Lloyd were rolling in the weeds, busting their guts laughing. Tansy shook her bundle of switches at me.

Chapter Four

Flowers for Miss Myrt

We stuck it out till daylight, me and Lloyd. When we could finally settle down, we slept in the bed of the spring wagon, plastered all over with oats. J.W. joined us and chased rabbits all night in his sleep, jerking continually.

We'd planned to sleep like cowboys around the fire but forgot to bring a length of rope to circle the campsite. A snake won't crawl over a rope. We slept in the wagon and left our trotlines behind where they were. What Charlie'd found on the hook discouraged us somewhat.

Charlie had seen Tansy home in the middle of the night. I suppose they'd come out to the crick together, and they went back together. They'd tied up Stentor down the road, out of sight.

It beat me how those two had come up with a plan to spook me so quick. For Pete's sake, Miss Myrt hadn't cooled before they'd cooked up a scheme. And she wasn't stiff before they scared the p-waddin' out of me. I blamed Tansy. She'd be the brains of the outfit.

But Charlie and Tansy? The two of them with their heads together was a new one on me.

By dawn's early light, Lloyd rode Siren into the crick to give her a drink. We hitched her to the wagon, poured water on the embers, and set off for home on the crown of the road.

"Hoo-boy," Lloyd said. Him and J.W. were up on the board, crowding me. "You shoulda had a look at your face. When you seen Tansy being the ghost of Miss Myrt, you went whiter than any sheet."

"You went bright green when you thought Charlie was Old Man Lichtenberger's ghost."

"I was just surprised," Lloyd said. "Then I tripped. I was cool as a cucumber."

"Same color as one too," I said. We rattled on behind Siren's switching tail.

Presently, Lloyd said, "It was worse for you."

"How come?" I said.

"Because Charlie's your pal."

That was pretty wise for a ten-year-old. Too wise, and it made me think. When a girl mixes into things, even Tansy, you don't know who your pals are, and that's the truth. I changed the subject, and then me and Lloyd voiced our hopes that they'd shut down Hominy Ridge School.

When we got home, Tansy was at the stove, looking way too solid to ever be a ghost. She was frying up a pan of eggs. "Go on down to the henhouse and see what you see," she said over her shoulder. She'd already gathered the eggs. They were there in two pails. "Go on," she said, and we went.

The Rhode Island Reds were in the yard, all down at one end standing on each other's heads. They were way too quiet and watchful. For two cents I wouldn't have approached the henhouse at all.

It was dim inside, and slick underfoot. We were just in the door when I skidded to a stop. There was a big, long bullsnake right there on the henhouse floor. Part of him. He'd crawled in through a knothole in the wall and tried to crawl out the same way.

But he'd swallowed an egg whole, and it made a lump in him that wouldn't let him fit through the knothole. He didn't have the sense to try another way out. You could see where he'd thrashed around, but now he was quiet, playing possum. Lloyd gaped around me at him. I guess we both gaped.

We went outside to see the rest of him. Seemed like we'd had about enough snakes for the time being. But ten or twelve inches of this one hung down the side of the henhouse with his mean-looking head in the dust.

We went for the ax and chopped him through at the

wall. "You want to cut the egg out of him?" Lloyd asked.

"You want to eat it?" I said, so we left it. We divvied up the snake with the ax for the hens to feed on and buried the head. I didn't see this as a bad sign at the time. Later I wondered.

There was a day between before Miss Myrt's funeral. That was about as long as you could wait on a funeral in this weather. But she had a brother coming from French Lick. The idea that a teacher would have a brother at all stumped Lloyd.

Baz Ellenbogen, who hadn't made it through the first reader under Miss Myrt some years back, was the grave digger. As Baz himself said, he never dug a grave he enjoyed more. But the day wasn't to be pure pleasure. Far from it. And I still think the snake in the henhouse was an evil omen of trouble coming.

On the morning of Miss Myrt's funeral, we hoed weeds in the field like troopers. But as quick as we knocked off for noon dinner, Tansy was all over us. We could not do anything right.

And we had to wear shoes and clean underdrawers to the funeral. Shoes on a weekday. Underdrawers in August. We fumed. I was too busy dodging Tansy's thumps to wonder why she couldn't just enjoy the day like everybody else. I'd be real glad to see her back in town for high school. She was getting awful hard to live with.

Then after dinner she sent us down to the garden to pick a big bunch of glads. "Flowers?" I said, dancing out of her range. "We're boys. We don't pick flowers."

"You'll be picking up your teeth if you don't." She made a fist.

Eyeing it, I said, "What for?"

"For Miss Myrt," Tansy snapped. "Show some respect for once. And make sure the colors don't clash. Don't take all day. I'd go myself, but I have a hat to trim, and I'm going to take a bath in the trough."

"A bath?" Lloyd's eyes bugged out. "It's *Thursday.*"

The next thing I knew, me and him were down in the garden, picking glads. "Do these clash?" Lloyd kept asking, waving every color at me.

"How would I know?" I said, squatting and grunting. I'd sooner hoe weeds. There's some dignity to that.

We labored on under the midday sun. Then Lloyd said, "We could pick all one color. Then they wouldn't clash."

"Yes," I sulked, "but nothing we ever do is right."

Chapter Five

A Mess of Bad Puppies

It was close and airless in the church before the female mourners got their cardboard fans going. Wasps droned in the window wells as people shuffled in, filling the pews. Us Culvers were down front, one pew back from the mourners' bench where Miss Myrt's brother from French Lick sat.

Dad wore his coat and his Sunday shirt with the detachable cuffs. His derby hat rested on his knee, turned up to show the puckered-silk lining. In his Sunday best and shaved, Dad was a fine-looking man. He could have passed for a judge.

Beneath a spray of entirely white glads, the lid on the pine coffin stood open before us. It was without question Miss Myrt Arbuckle laid out within. She had the longest nose in North America. It stood up against the yawning lid, shiny and sharp with a flaring nostril. She had a snout on her long enough to drink water down a crawdad hole.

Lloyd was all eyes, shifting around to see better until Dad laid a calming hand on him. I was about as near a corpse as I cared to be. Tansy loomed next to me. She'd trimmed her straw hat with a ribbon of funeral purple. Her feet were as big as mine, and I knew her shoes were crowding them painfully. Served her right for making me and Lloyd wear ours. Aunt Maud on her far side had a black veil pulled over her hat, and it made her look like a spider in its web.

This was the whole family. Our mother had died having Lloyd. Aunt Maud was Mother's sister. When he was a widower, Dad asked Aunt Maud to be his wife, to give us kids a mother. Or as Aunt Maud put it, "My number come up."

But she said she was nothing but a nervous spinster, and she didn't think marriage would calm her. Besides, she said her health wouldn't stand up to matrimony, that in fact she was not long for this world. Dad would be a widower again before he turned around.

Aunt Maud lived just down the road in the old Singleterry home place where her and Mother had grown up.

Charlie Parr was across the aisle with his ma. From the pain in his face, he had on shoes too. As I'd predicted to Lloyd, everybody turned out. The murmuring behind us was drowning out the wasps. People stood outside in the Balm of Gilead cemetery, to hear the service through the windows.

Doc Wilkinson was one of the pallbearers. As the saying goes, doctors bury their mistakes, and he may have been here to see it done. Doc rolled pills and busted boils and cut fishhooks out of us if we couldn't dig them out ourselves. If your bowels weren't regular, he'd dose you with his own Peristaltic Persuader. He signed death certificates and birthed all the babies except for the Tarbox family, who had an annual baby and no way to pay.

The fanning was at fever pitch now, and here came Imogene Lustbader down the aisle, clutching her music. She was Tansy's age, but didn't go to high school. Switching her skirts around the coffin and trying not to look in it, she settled on the bench and opened the piano. Us Methodists were saving for an organ.

Imogene, who was moon-faced and not good-looking, worked her hands and opened her sheet music. Then she crashed down on the keys with "Goodnight Down Here, Good Morning Up There." After that she played "Someday We'll Understand," then the popular "Who'll Be Next? Be Ready," and finally "The Old Rugged Cross," played with a cake-walk tempo because we'd started late. It was the same songs as a real funeral, though without the usual sobbing after "The Old Rugged Cross."

Preacher Parr had sat in his high-back chair at the front, stroking his cheek and drawing inspiration from Imogene's music. Now he climbed into the pulpit and looked us over. There was tragedy in his eyes, but he liked funerals better than weddings. As he often said, "Better tears now than tears later."

He seemed old to me, even for somebody's dad, and he had chin whiskers. He glanced out the bright windows, then boomed, "Even the sunshine is somber today, brothers and sisters, when we see Miss Myrt Arbuckle on her final journey, as she swaps semesters for eternity."

He had a preacher's voice, hollow and joyless. "Miss Myrt was not one of us," Preacher Parr recalled. "She served here only twenty-two years, a foreigner in our midst, as she came from up around Crawfordsville. She was an old maid and a teacher, so you couldn't call her a full member of our community. But we done the best by her we could."

The congregation shifted, hoping for some credit.

"Oh yes, we built the Hominy Ridge School, a modern weatherboarded structure for her comfort and convenience, all with volunteer labor we gladly give."

Tansy twitched.

"How many in this particular House of the Lord recollect the old schoolhouse that Hominy Ridge School replaced?"

Dad stirred.

"Yes, sisters and brothers, the old schoolhouse, the first schoolhouse—the log schoolhouse, with its stick chimbley daubed with clay."

That brought forth the first amen, in a cracked voice from the back. "Who remembers the winds of January whistling in through the chinks in them pine logs?"

"Yo!" said Dad suddenly, his hand aloft.

"Who remembers how we young chilrun brought moss and branches to school every blessed morning in vain attempts to stuff the cracks in them everlasting logs against the frigid fury of winters like we don't have anymore?"

An elderly chorus of amens followed.

"Who remembers the cold comfort of that open hearth before we built a new school with its patented front-loader chunk stove with isinglass winders?"

"We do!" chorused the oldsters. "We do!" Aunt Maud shook her cardboard fan in the air.

"And who remembers the time the skunk got down the chimbley, and we thought we could smoke him out, and we learned different?"

The church rocked with happy laughter.

"Yes, and who remembers the schoolmaster of them early years, him whose final resting place is right outside in the Balm of Gilead graveyard? Who remembers the terrible Increase Whittlesey of blessed memory?"

Dad winced.

"Increase Whittlesey, ten foot tall in his clawhammer

coat with the three-foot, inch-thick birchwood paddle in his mighty hand, and the braided rawhide whip just for the boys?"

Dad flinched.

The congregation was about ready to witness now. They were on the edge of their pews.

"And who remembers a time when chilrun *wanted* to learn?" Preacher Parr's mighty fist exploded on the pulpit. Charlie had inherited his dad's big fists.

"Who remembers when chilrun were *happy* to learn?" (Wham)

"Who remembers when chilrun were *eager* to learn?" (Wham)

Mrs. Darrell Embree jumped to her feet a pew behind us and called out, "Tell it like it was!"

"Sister, that's what I'm doin'," Preacher Parr retorted, leather-lunged. Dimly, I began to see how he operated. Nobody would miss Miss Myrt, so Preacher Parr got them to miss the good old days when the winters were worse and the kids were better. At a funeral you want to miss something.

He seemed to drift away and leave Miss Myrt's corpse in the dust, so to speak. But then he doubled back on her.

"It was twenty-two long school years ago when Miss Myrt Arbuckle first come among us. It was in that year she was set up in the new Hominy Ridge schoolhouse with its fresh-dug well, its pony shed, and its other necessary outbuildings. It was twenty-two years ago that the school board issued her first annual teaching supplies, a fresh box of chalk and a new broom.

"Who remembers the young woman come among us at that time? I don't know if you can say she was in the full bloom of her youth. I'm not sure the bloom was ever on Miss Myrt. And she was plain. That's the only word for her. As the saying goes, she was 'all wool and no embroidery.' But she was a great big robust woman. Why, it would have taken a wagon scale to weigh her and two trips to the grain elevator to get her there."

Preacher Parr fell suddenly silent. The afternoon sun sparked off the square specs riding down his nose. You could have heard a bee belch.

Then he pointed directly down into the coffin and its contents. "And look now at the wretched husk of that woman today!" he roared. "Look upon all that remains of her remains!"

The church creaked as people stood at the back for a better view.

"What brought her to this?" the preacher inquired. "She was a teacher of the old school, no doubt about it. Her motto was, 'No lickin', no larnin'.'"

"Amen to that!" several grown-ups echoed.

"She taught to the thwack of the hickory sprout," Preacher Parr remembered. "She done the best she could, so what cut her off in her prime, more or less?

"I ask you, sisters and brothers, what brought her low?

Doc Wilkinson tells me her poor heart just give out, and that's the scientific diagnosis. But who's to blame?

"We are a people of piety. We need somebody to blame." (Wham)

"Without blame, there is no shame." (Wham)

"Without shame, there is no humility!" (Double wham)

Preacher Parr shook a fist at heaven. "I'll ask you one more time. Who put this woman in her coffin before her span was up? Who sent her from the Here to the Hereafter on the milk train? Who punched her ticket untimely?"

The congregation pondered, and I had a bad feeling I knew who. So did Lloyd. He was still as a statue between me and Dad, trying to make himself smaller.

"That's right, mothers and fathers. Hear your hearts. It's the degraded chilrun of this modern age who put Miss Myrt down like a lame horse. Chilrun ruined by ease. Chilrun who think they have every right to sit by the stove and hog the heat while their ears are deaf to learning. Young gals with bright bows in their hussy hair. Young boys with impure thoughts gnawing at their vitals!"

It was amazing how small Lloyd could make himself. It was almost like there was nobody between me and Dad. I wished I could do that.

"The ungrateful!" (Wham)

"The unruly!" (Wham)

"The uncalled for!" (Wham)

"They are the authors of this woe! This generation of the young is one mess of bad puppies. Oh ye parents, take it out of their hides tonight! Rein them in before they strike again!"

Preacher Parr faltered and fell back. The amens liked to raise the roof. He put out a trembling hand to stem them. "I cain't go on in the face of this injustice," he said, husky-voiced, "the old at the mercy of the young. I turn to a finer spirit than I am, a greater talent than I possess."

We waited spellbound to hear who Preacher Parr thought better of than himself. "I refer to the Spirit of Poetry, who dwells anonymous among us. Dwelleth."

We murmured among ourselves.

"Yes, I'm talking to you about the Sweet Singer of Sycamore Township."

The murmurs mounted. There was for a fact a poet among us, somebody nobody knew. Every once in a while a poem would appear from the Sweet Singer. It might be topical. It might be seasonal. It might be a warning outright. You'd find it nailed to a tree or posted on the church door or sent to the Rockville newspaper. Nobody knew who the poet was. Everybody wondered, but nobody knew.

"And so as we see Miss Myrt off, I can do no better than to conclude with this poem from the Sweet Singer, come mysteriously to my attention." Clearing his throat, Preacher Parr intoned:

Alas, Miss Myrt has shuffled
off this sad and mortal coil,
Free at last from a spinster's lot
And a teacher's toil.

In her day she was never meek
And rarely if ever mild;
How well she knew that to spare the rod
Was to spoil the ignorant child.

We trusted her with our young'uns,
And for goodness sake
Some of the kids around here
Are meaner than a snake.

She was plainer than a pikestaff
And rougher than a cob,
But at her sad departure
We all fetch up a sob.

Though we take a solemn solace
That in the sweet by and by
Miss Myrt's a-cuttin' switches
For that Schoolhouse in the Sky.

Sincerely yours,
The Sweet Singer of Sycamore Township

A reverential silence lingered. Then Mrs. Darrell Embree called out, "The Sweet Singer has hit the nail on the head with that one! It is the finest piece of literature written in our lifetime!"

Cries rose from around the church:

"Beautiful!"

"Touching!"

"Shakespeare, move over!"

I stole a look at Tansy. She didn't seem to think much of the poem. So I guessed she wasn't the Sweet Singer. Now we knew Miss Myrt wasn't either, though nobody would have accused her of having any poetry in her soul.

The Sweet Singer's poem took the place of the concluding prayer. We were on the home stretch now. Down the aisle came Albertine Winchell, another girl about Tansy's age. She swept around the coffin and Imogene, and mounted the steps to the altar. Turning on us, she cupped her hands and burst into song: "Not Lost But Gone Before," with piano accompaniment.

To these strains us mourners began to troop down for a final farewell to Miss Myrt, starting from the rear. Everybody we knew jostled down the aisle, except of course for the Tarbox clan and Aunt Fanny Hamline, who were naturally not there.

At last our pew stood over the coffin. Aunt Maud's black-gloved hand clutched the coffin rim and she shook her veils at the corpse. "Mine will be the next face they shovel the dirt on," she said in prophecy.

They hadn't been able to brush all the chalk dust out of Miss Myrt's dress, so she looked natural. Somebody had tucked her gradebook into a breast pocket.

"Oh for pity's sake!" Tansy said pretty loud. "Who put that pointer in her hand? Honest-to-Pete!"

Clutched in both Miss Myrt's waxen hands was the pointer she slapped the map with or pointed to things with on the blackboard. She never whupped us with it because it was too valuable: a fine polished maple shaft with a brass bullet tip.

To the great astonishment of me and Lloyd and probably Dad, Tansy barked, "They aren't going to put that pointer in the ground. It's worth good money, and there's plenty of use left in it!"

With that, Tansy turned back her cuffs and reached into the coffin to work the pointer loose from Miss Myrt's clenched hands. It slid right out, but one of her knuckles seemed to jerk, and my knees buckled. If Miss Myrt had grabbed for that pointer and hung on to take it with her to the Schoolhouse in the Sky, I'd have passed right out on the spot. And Lloyd too, though he was so small now, he could barely see into the coffin.

The pointer was in Tansy's fist. She was stalking out the side door of the church. Her big straw hat quivered with purpose. You talk about an evil omen.

That moment had trouble written all over it.

Chapter Six

The First Such Mishap of the Twentieth Century

Bad omens abounded, and we didn't get home from Miss Myrt's funeral without another one. Quite a big one.

Dad owned a good buggy, made by the Durant-Dort Carriage Company with a collapsible leather roof. It carried only two people, though, especially if one of you was Tansy. So it didn't get much use.

We'd gone to the funeral in the spring wagon drawn by Siren and Stentor. Coming home, Lloyd and Dad were up on the board. Clinging to the sides, Tansy and Aunt Maud stood in the wagon bed with me and J.W. He naturally went too. You couldn't leave home without him. The roads were graveled and pretty good between the church and our place, and it was getting past the heat of the day.

We were coming up to the crossing of Quagmire Road and the Hog Scald Road, where there's a high screen of hedge apple. I for one heard something like summer thunder.

Stentor and Siren were just about to make the turn onto Hog Scald Road when there came a terrible banshee scream. Both horses reared and liked to fall back on Lloyd and Dad. Polished metal flashed. I thought of the all-steel Case Agitator. Then we had one rear wheel down in the ditch, and the wagon hung at a steep angle.

There were oats in my mouth as I slid down the bed. J.W. skidded and scrabbled beside me. Dad seemed to be on the board still, clinging to the reins. Lloyd did a backflip and lit on Tansy. The two of them, loosely bunched, slid down too.

Above us, Dad fought to keep the horses from breaking out and bolting. I hit the backboard with a thump, and J.W. was all over me. Tansy and Lloyd hit with a bigger thump. Me and J.W. piled out of one side of the wagon, Tansy and Lloyd the other. Tansy's hat with the funeral ribbon was still on her head because of the hatpins, but askew, and ruined. A moment of stunned silence fell.

Then Tansy hollered, "Where's Aunt Maud?"

A second before, Aunt Maud had been clinging to the wagon side, jigging home with the rest of us. Now she seemed to have taken flight. I looked up in the hedge apple trees to see if she'd flown up there. But Tansy was skittering down the slick weeds toward the ditch. It was deep, and there was standing water in it.

Then we saw Aunt Maud's black veil draped over a sticker bush. Beyond it, between weeds and water, Aunt Maud herself was stretched out in a bed of cress.

Her skirts were over her head. The elastic of her summer drawers gripped her thighs. Then came blue-white knees. Then black stockings, rolled over garters, down to her high-topped, year-round Sunday-and-funeral shoes. It was more of Aunt Maud than I had ever seen. Lloyd too. J.W. pulled back at the sight of her and drew up one paw.

"Aunty, Aunty, can you hear me?" Tansy cried, tangling her skirts in the sticker bush.

"I'm a dead woman." Aunt Maud's voice was muffled by her skirts. "Didn't I say I'd be next? Lay me out." She sat up, sweeping down her skirts, and she too still had on her hat.

I marveled at how far she'd lit from the wagon. She must have done a double somersault off the backboard.

"Is everybody all right?" Dad called from above us. "Had I better come down?" But he had his hands full with the panicky horses.

I scrambled up the bank to tell him we were all fine and Aunt Maud had won for distance.

When I reached him, Dad was beside Siren, soothing her. She and Stentor were starting to settle. Dad was standing almost at his ease, talking to a stranger. He was a young man, suddenly appeared, who seemed to be off some other planet. He wore a helmet with goggles pushed up and leather leggings.

Behind him, half in the far ditch on Hog Scald Road, was a sight I couldn't get my eyes around. It was an automobile. Not our first. We'd seen a couple in town, a curved-dash Oldsmobile, for one. But nothing like this. This one was long and lean, like a dream of a driving machine. It was a racing car. Now Lloyd and J.W. were beside me, drinking it all in.

The young man who'd nearly run us down was named Eugene Hammond. Him and Dad had already exchanged names and decided it had been a near miss with no real harm done on either side.

"Go ahead," Eugene Hammond said to me and Lloyd. "You can have a look at it." He knew we itched to get closer. We crept across the road. I was still spitting oats. J.W. wasn't sure, but didn't want to be left out.

The car was warm to the touch like a living thing. I'd heard its roar and thought it was thunder. I'd heard its screaming brakes and thought of banshees. Its balloon tires were so thick, you couldn't span them with your hand, and the machine steered with another wheel. A double seat, but no roof to catch the wind. Nothing between the driver and any distance, nowhere to go but ahead.

It was the "Bullet No. 2" racing car, the first with an eight-cylinder, in-line engine, according to Eugene Hammond. Him and Dad had drifted across the road too, as Dad was drawn to the machine. The famous Barney Oldfield had driven this car last winter at Daytona Beach, Florida. He'd traveled a mile in forty-three seconds. It made me dizzy to hear, and Lloyd caught his breath. Dad looked a little skeptical. He pulled on his chin. Dad's where Lloyd gets that gesture.

"I see your wagon was made by the Standard Wheel Company of Terre Haute, Mr. Culver."

"It's a pretty good wagon when it's not in the ditch," Dad said.

"It was the top of our wagon line," Eugene Hammond said.

"You're associated with the Standard Wheel Company?" Dad asked.

"I am, though we're switching our operations over to motor carriage manufacture. We'll be the Overland Automobile Company. I'm showing the Bullet No. 2 at fairs throughout Indiana to advertise our company. It's the coming thing, Mr. Culver. As a farmer, you see its possibilities. You'll have heard that the P. H. Studebaker Company at South Bend is moving over to autos, and they're a bigger operation than we are."

Things were moving too fast for Dad. His mind was still back in Terre Haute. "You don't mean to tell me you come from Terre Haute in that thing today." Dad touched a tire. A pneumatic tire.

"Mr. Culver," Eugene Hammond said, "I could have come from Evansville today in that thing."

Dad went ashen.

"I could have come from Louisville, Kentucky."

It was a moment of near-religious wonder.

And it was soon over. Aunt Maud showed up in the road, leaning on Tansy. "Well, if that ain't men all over! Talking machinery when I could be dead in that ditch!" Aunt Maud vibrated through her veil. "If it hadn't been for this girl here who had to about carry me up the bank on her back, I'd still be in the cress down there, wilting like a salad with one foot in the cattails and the other in the grave!"

Tansy caught her first sight of Eugene Hammond. Her hand stole up to the broken brim of her hat. Eugene Hammond noticed her too, saying to Dad, "I hope the young lady suffered no injury." He'd pulled off his driving gloves to shake hands with Dad. The gloves hung loose in his grip, yellow wash-leather gloves with buckles.

"Mercy, no." Tansy spoke in a voice unfamiliar to us. "I was but momentarily discommoded." We all stared at her new vocabulary. Lloyd gaped. The broken brim on her hat hung down over one of her ears, and stickers had snagged her skirts. She wasn't looking her best.

It was time to be on our way. Eugene Hammond joined us behind the wagon to help the horses drag it back on the road. Aunt Maud supervised. She claimed she might be too nervous ever to get back in any wagon. But when Eugene Hammond offered to deliver her home in his racing car, she bellered like a calf and vaulted into the wagon bed unaided.

We found Dad's derby hat undented. It was on his head now. He was up on the board again with the reins in his hand. We were about to part company with Eugene Hammond, who said, "Mr. Culver, I hope the next time our paths cross, the circumstances will not be so sudden. But we may have made history today."

Dad wondered how.

"I daresay this is the first mishap between horse-drawn vehicle and automobile in rural Parke County in the twentieth century, or in fact human history."

Dad allowed that it was entirely possible.

Tansy stood backward in the wagon as we went off down the Hog Scald Road. She watched the fine figure of Eugene Hammond cranking his Bullet No. 2 until he was lost in the distance. She adjusted her hat, but the brim came off in her hand.

The whole experience recalled to Dad the first time an automobile had turned up in this district. Four, five years ago nobody around here had ever seen one. Then one day a car came down the road past the Ogilvy place.

Harve and Orv Ogilvy, father and son, were out in their field. They were both dumber than stumps. When they saw that automobile coming in the distance, they didn't know what it was. Harve ran for his gun. When he got back, the car was closer, so Harve fired both barrels at it. The car swerved out of the ruts and came to a halt. The driver jumped down and vanished into a stand of broom-corn.

"Did you kill that thing, Paw?" Orv asked Harve.

"No," Harve said, "but I got him to turn loose of the man he had hold of."

Anyway it's how the story went, and we told it again, jigging on home past ditches bright with daylilies. J.W. barked us by all our neighbors and their livestock. It seemed to me that about everything that could ever happen in an August already had.

That night after an early supper, the school board met in an emergency meeting. They had to decide what to do about Hominy Ridge School now that Miss Myrt was in the ground. They were meeting down in our parlor.

It wasn't quite dark outside, after a long day. Me and Lloyd were already upstairs in our room. We'd shoved the big brass bed we shared into the bay window, hoping a breath of cool night air would make a wrong turn and stumble across us.

Lloyd was already in bed, in one of Dad's old Sunday

shirts he wore for a nightshirt in this weather. He had a tin button pinned on it with the J. I. Case threshing-machine eagle. I was stretched out with an ear applied to the floor, trying to listen in on the school board meeting below. All I heard was a mumbling buzz.

From the bed Lloyd said, "Russell, you think Dad's going to take it out of our hide for killing Miss Myrt?"

"Shut up, I'm trying to hear the school board," I pointed out. "Don't you want to know if they're closing down the school?"

"You can't hear anything," Lloyd said. "You think Dad's going to take it out of our—"

"No, it was just a funeral oration, which is no different than a sermon," I said. "Dad knows we didn't kill Miss Myrt. She died of her own meanness. The bile backed up in her, and she foundered on it."

I knew Lloyd was up there in the middle of the mattress, pulling on his chin, being skeptical.

"Besides, when did Dad ever take anything out of your hide?" I said. "When did he ever once whup you?"

"That time you got me to steal his .22 rifle to kill rats in the barn, and I shot Siren instead, and she kicked the door off her stall."

"Well," I said, "other than that."

"The time you got me to plug every watermelon in the patch to find the ripest one, and we ruined a whole wagonload of—"

"Well," I said, "if you don't count—"

"The time you—"

"All right," I said, "all right. But Dad's not going to do anything, so forget all about it. Put it out of your mind. We're innocent."

"That's what you said the time we—"

"Lloyd, don't make me come up there and hide you myself."

I strained in vain to hear the direction the meeting was taking. Still, it was cooler here on the floor. Time passed.

"Russell," came a small voice from the bed, "what's the prettiest thing you ever seen?"

I sighed. "I don't know. It sure wasn't Aunt Maud with her skirts over her head."

"But what was?"

"I guess the new steel Case Agitator threshing machine."

Silence from the bed. After a couple minutes I said, "What's the prettiest thing you ever seen?"

"That Bullet No. 2 racing car," Lloyd said, just waiting to be asked.

I saw what he meant. That thing seemed to be moving and on the prowl even when it was tipped into the ditch. It was like a knife you could cut through time, a hole you could punch in the universe. It was like fast in a shape. It might have been prettier than the Case Agitator.

My ear was taking root to the floor. I couldn't hear anything informative, but I was getting tired enough to sleep right here where I'd dropped.

Finally Lloyd said, "You know the prettiest thing Tansy ever seen?"

"No. Do you?"

"I bet I know."

"What?" I said.

"Eugene Hammond," Lloyd said. Then he dropped right off. His breathing rose and fell, regular. Probably when I was a kid, I dropped off that quick too.

The voices rumbled below me. It was night now with moonlight on the floor. Then I heard another voice, higher-pitched, mingling with the low. A voice of the female sex, and it wasn't Aunt Maud. We'd taken her home.

That left Tansy. Tansy and the school board.

It took me a minute. Then I had goose bumps all over like somebody had trod on my grave. Suddenly I pictured Tansy with Miss Myrt's pointer in her grip. Somewhere in my head Tansy slapped a map. I had the evidence of my ear. The terrible truth dawned on me by moonlight. All those evil omens had led to this. I shook like a wet dog.

My pouncing thoughts would run me crazy if I didn't do something. I couldn't wake Lloyd and tell him. I dared not put it into words. But to ease my mind, I could spook him. Spooking the p-waddin' out of him almost always made me feel better. "Lloyd, you asleep?" I asked, loud enough to wake him.

"What," he mumbled.

"I was just thinking," I said in a thoughtful voice.

"What about?"

"Miss Myrt. With that nose on her, I wonder if they got the coffin lid down."

"Oh."

"And about Increase Whittlesey, of course."

"Who?"

"Didn't you hear anything at the funeral? He was the old schoolmaster before Miss Myrt's time. Ten foot tall in his clawhammer coat."

"So what?"

"Well, this is the first night Miss Myrt's in her grave. Now Increase Whittlesey's not the only teacher in the graveyard, pushing up daisies."

"So what?" Lloyd said again.

"So it could make him restless. He could feel crowded. It could make him . . . walk by night. I thought I saw his shadow on the ceiling. I bet if you looked out the window, you might could see—"

"Oh, shut up, Russell." Lloyd turned over, and I was alone with my terrible, pouncing thoughts. Sleep was out of the question now, and I dreaded daylight.

Chapter Seven

A Droning of Locusts, a Mourning of Doves

In time, the locust drone of the school board gave over to the mourning of doves in the eaves. I suppose I dozed. Pale light showed in the east. But I didn't dream until after the rooster crowed. Then I was up to my knees in long-distance Dakota wheat fields, a sea of wheat bent by the breeze, halfway to harvest.

I was bolt awake now, sitting up on the bedroom floor, ripped from sleep by a smell from the kitchen. I couldn't believe the evidence of my nose. It was mush frying. Cornmeal mush. Hanging over it was the sweetness of sorghum molasses coming to the boil.

Lloyd sat up in bed. "Did we oversleep?" he said, groggy, smelling the air. "Is it a school day?"

Because we never had fried mush till school started.

Here we were, clinging to the last shard and shred of summertime, while downstairs Tansy was frying up mush like it was September. Like she couldn't hardly wait.

Then I remembered.

We pulled on our overalls. Lloyd was towheaded, and his head looked like a haystack this morning. I didn't have the heart to ride him about it, or tell him the news. Let him find out in his own good time. Let it come as a shock to him too. Just to make this like any old morning, I tried to trip him at the top of the stairs. He skipped out of my way as usual.

We went to milk, but didn't tarry. You can only milk so fast, but we didn't horse around, squirting milk into each other's mouth and such as that. We milked out our half and turned the calves in for theirs and made for the house for our breakfast.

Dad was at his place at the table. Aunt Maud was just coming up the back porch. On the road between her place and ours she smoked a cob pipe every morning. But she never smoked before witnesses. You could hear her bang the ash out on the steps.

"She's going to burn the porch off the house one of these times," Dad often remarked.

Aunt Maud stalked into the kitchen. "That tumble I took out of the wagon yesterday shook loose every bone in my body," she said. "If I sneeze, I'll fly apart."

Tansy was rounding the table with our plates of

breakfast up her arm. She ended behind Lloyd and gave the back of his haystack a painful thump.

"Ow!"

"Do you have such a thing as a comb upstairs?" Tansy inquired. Me and him shared a comb, and I'd had the sense to use it this morning.

"You go around looking like one of the Tarbox clan," Tansy said.

"It's still summer," said Lloyd, who never knew when to button his lip. "Who's looking?"

Playing fair, Tansy gave me a painful thump too since she was still back there, handy to our heads.

"Ow!" I said. "I didn't do nothing."

"You didn't do *anything*." Tansy leaned into my ear. "We're going to do something about your grammar this year. You talk like a Hoosier hayseed. And we're going to have a look at your orthography."

The thought of Tansy having a look at my orthography brought me near tears. It was almost the last thing you'd want a sister looking at. Dad was gazing away out the door, down the corn rows. He was on the school board. He could have put a stop to this.

"Let's see those hands." Tansy poked Lloyd. "And a clean handkerchief. It can be ragged, but you better hope it's clean."

"A clean handkerchief?" Lloyd said. "What is this, sch—"

It hit him like a ton of bricks. His eyes were already watery from the thump. Now they welled up. "No," he whispered. "Say it ain't so."

But it was.

In their wisdom, the school board had hired on Tansy to take Miss Myrt's place at Hominy Ridge School. They wouldn't pay for a real teacher trained at the Terre Haute normal school. Probably Miss Myrt herself had never darkened the door of the normal school, or even been to Terre Haute. They could get Tansy for thirty-six dollars a month because she still had a year of high school to go. She'd no doubt talked them into it. But it wouldn't have taken much. The school board dearly loved a bargain.

Seemed to me if they filled in the privies, locked up the school, and threw the key down the well, they could save some real money and do us all a service. But the school board was deaf to reason. Dad stared down the corn rows, hearing nothing.

Lloyd whimpered.

The mush was ashes in my mouth. But I was sure of my plan now. As quick as we got the potatoes dug and the winter wheat planted and I had a little money put aside, I'd be off to the Dakotas for the harvest. Me and Charlie Parr.

It was Lloyd I felt sorry for. I was going to get out of here or know the reason why. He was just a kid and had to stay. My heart went out to him. Tansy'd have him thumped senseless by Christmas.

"But what does she even know?" he said beside me in a small voice.

We never knew what she'd learned at high school. We wondered.

"They let you be teacher," I mumbled back, "if you can count to twenty with your shoes on."

"Quit that mumbling and eat," Tansy barked from the stove.

"Amen to that," echoed Aunt Maud.

What's the hurry? We soon learned.

We'd meant to mow hay. We had twelve acres of alfalfa with timothy and red clover mixed in and some wild stuff that seeded itself. I liked mowing. It made a change from weeding, and the barn swallows followed to catch the bugs the mower scared up, so you weren't eaten alive.

But Dad said, "After you boys see to the stock, take the morning off and walk down to the schoolhouse with your sister. Find out what needs to be done down there." Dad didn't look right at us. "The hay'll wait on you." Then he made his escape.

We slumped.

Tansy and Aunt Maud were back and forth between dish-board and stove, laying the groundwork for dinner. The whole deal kept dawning on me. Tansy wouldn't be in Rockville for high school, so we'd have her day and night. But being teacher, she'd have to leave the cooking to Aunt Maud. It was the worst of two worlds.

Lloyd fetched up a sigh with a sob in it.

The three of us, me and Lloyd and Tansy, hoofed it down the Hog Scald Road to school. It was only about a mile, and uphill both ways, as the road to school always was back then. And we were barefoot, as we were all winter in our memories later. J.W. came too. He was regular in his school attendance and supposed this was the first day.

They hadn't issued Tansy her box of chalk and new broom yet. She carried a bucket and a scrub brush from home. I had a scythe for the weeds. Lloyd was chunking rocks at fence posts and diving in and out of the ditch with J.W. The ditches were thronged with elderberry and dark with patches of mint down low. Lloyd would pop up out of the ditch, chewing mint. He seemed to be in danger of forgetting the seriousness of the occasion.

I was too sulky to speak and took my mind off my troubles by recalling how Hog Scald Road got its name.

In pioneer days there was said to be a boiling spring around here. The early settlers ran their hogs into that boiling spring and let them jump out when they were half cooked. Then the farmers drove the hogs through a nettle hedge, so they were scalded and scraped all at once and ready to be gutted and carved into cutlets and tongue.

And if you believe that one, I'll tell you another. I liked pig stories better than pigs. In fact, I didn't care much for livestock of any kind.

The nearer to school, the better Tansy's posture. She was ramrod straight. Was she getting up her courage?

The schoolhouse had lost some shingles and had the dry, webby look of a schoolhouse in summertime. Ragweed had taken the yard and tangled the privy paths. Somebody had sawed through a post on the pony shed. The door on the woodshed hung from a single hinge.

A plank was laid over the ditch to the front step. Tansy put her bucket down and stroked her throat in a thoughtful, womanly way. We both looked up at the bell tower. You could see from here the rope was gone. You couldn't expect a bell rope to last the summer. Somebody would want it for plow lines.

Tansy counted silently on her fingers.

"What?" I said.

"The kids," she said. "How many are we going to have?"

Well, there was me and Charlie Parr, at least for the time being. And Lloyd and Lester Kriegbaum and Flopears Lumley and Pearl Nearing. Six, unless there'd be new ones. We'd graduated three in the spring. And two or three had fallen by the wayside over last year. Orv Ogilvy had lit out for the Dakotas.

"We'll need eight," Tansy murmured.

"What?"

"I said we'll need eight," she snapped.

"Why?"

"Because the school board won't keep school for any fewer."

Oh, I thought, hope dawning.

They'd issued Tansy the key, but somebody had bunged in the lock with a stove length. The door swung open to a push. The lock was on the floor among splinters. We stepped into the coat room under the bell tower. There were nails for the boys' hats on one side and nails for the girls' on the other. And shelves for our dinner pails. The place smelled real bad, a warmed-over stink of mothballs and something like sheep dip.

Over the door to the schoolroom were nailed a pair of brackets. Miss Myrt stretched a beech switch up there, about four foot long, very supple and whippy. Us pupils walked in under this switch every blessed morning, and it was to put us in the right frame of mind for learning.

I followed Tansy into the schoolroom, which smelled worse. It wasn't a big room, a little longer than it was wide. A row of windows on either side were set too high to see out of, so we couldn't be distracted by the world. The desks were modern with inkwells, though carved up. Down front was the recitation bench, backless.

On a platform called the rostrum was Miss Myrt's—teacher's—desk. The bracket that held the map was there, but somebody had swiped the map itself, a good cloth-backed one with a lot of uses. The mud wasps had built their big nest against a ceiling rafter.

It was just the two of us in the schoolroom. Lloyd loitered outside with J.W. I had an awful vision of being up on the recitation bench with nothing between me and Tansy riding her desk like a bronco and cracking a beech switch in the air like a carriage whip. My mind shuddered.

"Tansy, what do you even know?" I braced for a thump.

"More than you," she replied. A shadow crossed her eyes. "But I'll be examined." I'd never heard her unsure.

"What?"

"The County Superintendent of Schools will examine my . . . abilities. I'll need a certificate."

"Tansy, why do you even want to be a teacher? It don't seem like good, honest work to me."

She gave me a sidelong glance. "You'll find out in the fullness of time."

"Fullness of time" sounded like the way they probably talk at the high school.

At least there was some air in here. Three of the window lights were broken out. There were rocks on desks among the petrified yellow jackets, and glass on the floor right where you wanted to step.

"Tarboxes," Tansy said.

I thought so too, though I doubted they'd stolen the bell rope for plow lines. They plowed but little. Still, the busted lock and the window lights and the missing map had Tarbox written all over them. Me and Tansy both looked at the library shelved under the windows. All six books were there, so it was Tarboxes for sure. They never went near books.

The hogs had clearly gotten in too, and that meant fleas.

"But no animal done that." I pointed to a corner.

"No animal *did* that," Tansy said, handing me the bucket.

Me and Lloyd went for water and took our sweet time about it. We fell over J.W. in both directions. He'd taken up residence on the front step and was scanning the road, wondering where everybody was.

The evening before school took up, me and Dad and Lloyd and J.W. rode down to the schoolhouse in the wagon with the long ladder from the barn. I was up on the board beside Dad with half an old bedsheet wrapped around my middle, hidden under my shirt.

It was an ideal evening without a hint of fall in it.

As warm as July, too warm to be bound up like a mummy under my shirt. The hedges burgeoned, and the fields were heavy with bounty. It was an evening to inspire songs in praise of Indiana, of moonlight fair along the Wabash and the breath of new-mown hay from the fields and candlelight gleaming through sycamores.

"Pretty country," Dad said.

And it was, though nothing I couldn't leave behind as quick as I could get away. "Up in the Dakotas, some of them farms are so big, they have their own stern-wheel steamboats to carry their wheat to their own elevators at Fargo," I told Dad.

"You don't say," he remarked. "That's a big-scale operation."

We patched the lock on the front door. Then Dad planted the ladder in the coat room and climbed up to hang a new bell rope. He put in new window lights too, from glass we had on hand. He was an artist with a glass cutter. He could look at an opening and cut the pane to fit. There wasn't anything he couldn't do. The skill lived in his hands.

When it was time to head home, he said to me, "You going to need this ladder?"

"Dad," I said, "I am."

"Well, lock up behind you," he said. "And you and Lloyd can tote the ladder home between you. It's heavy, but I guess it's worth it to you. I'm making for home now. I don't want to know." He snapped his fingers. "All right, J.W., walkin' or ridin'?"

J.W. decided to ride with Dad, rather than hoof it with me and Lloyd. We watched the wagon out of sight, Dad high on the board, J.W. at his side. I unwound the old sheet from around my middle, and me and Lloyd climbed the ladder to the bell tower like two squirrels up a shellbark hickory. Careful not to ring it, I wrapped the old sheet around and around the clapper till it was stuffed tight within the bell. You could yank on that rope from now till New Year's and not get a tinkle.

"'Curfew must not ring tonight,'" I said down to Lloyd on the ladder below me. This was a one-man job, but he wanted in on it.

"I thought it wasn't supposed to ring tomorrow," he said.

"'Curfew must not ring tonight' is out of a poem. I'm quoting."

"Oh," said Lloyd. "Did the Sweet Singer write it?"

"Maybe. I don't know."

Anyway, when Tansy went to ringing that bell in the morning to call us inside, she'd get nothing but a muffled thump. It seemed like the least we could do for her first day.

It was pretty nearly dark on our way home. Because of the ladder, we took it easy and rested every whipstitch.

"Russell, I believe Dad knew we were up to something with this ladder."

"I think he did," I said.

"How'd he figure we were going to pull something on Tansy for her first day?"

"You got me. Maybe it was the sheet. It gave me a new shape. Maybe Dad just knows how we think."

The locusts were tuning up, and we walked on wordless a rod or two. Then Lloyd said, "You think Tansy knows how we think too?"

"She might."

"That's what I'm afraid of," Lloyd said in a small, sorry voice. "That's what's got me worried." We walked on home with the ladder, stepping high over shadows, in a drone of locusts and the gathering gloom, the night before school took up.

Part II

The Jailhouse of School

✯ ✯ ✯

Chapter Eight

Called to the Trough of Knowledge

As arranged, me and Charlie Parr met early that next morning behind the boys' privy. Our plan was to start out the school year by smoking a three-inch length of buggy whip.

I say early, but Tansy went off to school earlier still, along with her pointer and a new hat.

There was some mystery about the hat, though I gave but little thought to what women wore. It had turned up that morning in a fancy box on the porch. Dad brought it in when he came from plowing in the oat stubble. Tansy untied the fine ribbon and took off the lid and peered into the tissue paper inside. Then she drew out a hat.

Her breath stopped and tears formed in her eyes. It

looked to be quite a good hat, with grapes on it, better than the one that got busted up in the accident. I'd have personally thought it was a three-dollar hat.

"Why, Dad," she said carefully, "many thanks. It's elegant."

Dad opened his mouth to speak, but him and Tansy exchanged a glance, and he said nothing. Aunt Maud watched them both, narrow-eyed and thoughtful. And that's all there was to that.

Tansy put on her hat, and Dad took her to school in the wagon for her first day. Me and Lloyd would hoof it. Catch us turning up at school alongside the teacher! We made the pigs last till Dad and Tansy were off the place.

Another thing I liked about summer was that the pigs foraged free. You had to bring in the cows and milk them, but pigs saw to themselves. You just had to be sure they found water. Then you walked the shared fence lines to watch they didn't get through to root up your neighbor's pasture. That's all there was to it. The old sow would farrow her young in the out-of-doors. They'd spend their days at leisure in the hog wallow and nest in dry leaves by night. They liked summer better than being penned up. That's where me and pigs agreed.

"Dagnab it, I forgot matches," Charlie said with the buggy whip already between his teeth.

But I knew he would and drew a couple out of my overall pocket. He lit up. We were to our kneecaps in weeds and pods back here because I hadn't worked this far with the scythe.

From our outpost behind the privy we could see Lester and Lloyd and Flopears standing around in the yard, throwing their pocketknives at the ground. Lester wore short pants and a Buster Brown collar that could spell trouble for him in a bigger school. Flopears wore a patchwork shirt made out of old Bull Durham sacks. Lester was a bookworm, and Flopears could just about read, though he had to point at each word. Lloyd was somewhere in the middle. They were all around the same age.

"You get the bell wadded?" Charlie inquired, inhaling.

"I got that bell wadded tighter than a tick. Tansy wants us in school, she'll have to come out and pick us off one by one."

Charlie exhaled black smoke. "Boy, that's buggy whip!" he said, and passed the smoldering mess to me.

Pearl Nearing was making for the girls' privy. I nearly took her for a newcomer. She'd be about eleven, twelve, and she'd shot up over the summer. Though the smoke cut Charlie's eyes, he squinted through it at Pearl.

"Don't she have a different shape up above?" he wondered, and she seemed to. In the spring she was a skinny little thing who'd jump in puddles. Now she simpered along and picked her way to the privy, prissy.

She swung open the door to step in, screeched, and tripped herself backing out. "Who do you think you are?" she hollered into the privy, planting her fists on her new hips.

Me and Charlie watched. I wasn't inhaling the buggy whip. I didn't want to see my breakfast again. Not Aunt Maud's mush.

By and by, a small bonneted figure crept forth from the girls' privy. Her skirts were tucked up by mistake into her drawers behind. She didn't look hardly old enough for school, and she'd been crying.

"Well, what did you think you were doing in there?" Pearl demanded. "You weren't using it. You'd yanked up your drawers."

She'd been hiding in there, as any fool could see. You could tell from here her little chin was quivering.

"That makes seven of us," I said to Charlie, "unless she's a minnow we have to throw back."

"Ah," said Charlie, whose arithmetic never added up to much.

To my consternation, we heard a bell ring. It jangled the morning and summoned us to school. It wasn't the bell-tower bell. I'd seen to that. It was a cowbell. Tansy'd be standing smug in the front door, calling us cattle to the trough of knowledge.

"I blame Dad," I told Charlie. "He let me use the ladder to wad the bell. Then he must of give Tansy a cowbell from the milking parlor to even the score. He was playing fair again."

"Ah," said Charlie Parr through a screen of smoke.

In the olden days of schoolmaster Increase Whittlesey, the girls sat on one side, the boys on the other. The old chinky log schoolhouse had separate entrances for the sexes.

It was like that this morning. Pearl sat as far from us boys as she could get. Lester and Lloyd and Flopears were in a bunch at the same desk. For Lloyd's school haircut Aunt Maud had used the same bowl she used on me. She cut our hair by moonlight so it wouldn't grow so fast. Lloyd looked like a toadstool between Lester and Flopears. I must have looked similar.

Me and Charlie Parr sat close enough to converse on the back row. Even for the first day, he was almost suspiciously well barbered. His neck was shaved far above his shirt. He'd even shaved his face. His chin was smooth as a baby's bottom.

In those days it wasn't unusual to find scholars of twenty and even twenty-five doubling back for more schooling. They were liable to be older and meaner than the teacher. Some of them returned when they found out that if you couldn't sign your name, you had to pay cash. But today, me and Charlie were the old men of the group.

Even seen from back here, Tansy loomed large on the rostrum. It seemed to bow beneath her. Though she wasn't a welcome sight to me, I admit she cut a teacherish figure. She was strictly business in a starchy shirtwaist and shoes. Her hair was up, and that made her an adult right there. She was sure big enough to be a teacher—husband-high, as we said back then. And then some. Husband-high and teacher-tall. In her hand was the same pointer she'd dragged from the death grip of Miss Myrt.

The pointer had passed.

But you could tell Tansy didn't know where to begin. With a wobble in her voice, she said, "Good morning, pupils."

"Morning, Miss Myrt!" Flopears sang out because change came slow to him.

"Hey, Tansy," some said.

"Miss Tansy," she said.

I was condemned to eternal perdition if I was going to be able to call my own sister "Miss Tansy."

She'd made a note and consulted it. "All right," she said, "rules.

"There'll be no marble playing inside the schoolhouse, even in bad weather, and there'll be no playing for keeps, anywhere."

That law was directed to Lloyd and Lester and Flopears.

"Number two," Tansy said. "Chewing gum is strictly forbidden." Chewing gum was a girly thing to do. No boy would, so this rule was aimed at you-know-who.

Tansy faltered then, seeming to have only two rules.

"Right about now we generally sing," Charlie prompted.

Tansy raised her pointer, and we broke into our usual,

When bright the day is breaking,
And school day bells are waking,
With joy our homes forsaking,
We hail our pleasant school.

This was far from my favorite song, but Miss Myrt always made us start the day with it, often conducting with a switch. Charlie had a pretty fair baritone.

Now Tansy wracked her brain for what came next. She cleared her throat and counted us, but it took up very little time. *Six,* we all saw her say silently.

"And one in the privy!" Charlie sang out.

Shut up, Charlie, I thought. If there aren't enough of us, maybe we could just call it quits right—

"In the privy! Who's in the privy?"

All us boys turned up our hands. It wasn't our privy. Tansy turned on Pearl.

"Just some little chit of a girl," Pearl pouted, "and she has nothing to do with me."

"Go get her."

Any boy in the room would gladly go, just to get outdoors. Pearl smoothed her skirts and pulled in her lips. "Getting her is not my job, and you're not the boss of me, Tansy. I remember when you were one of us, and how long you took to get through the third reader." Pearl preened.

Tansy's eyes closed to a pair of dangerous slits. She stepped heavily down from the rostrum and pointed the polished pointer at Pearl. It came *this close* to her nose.

"Get her."

We all watched while Pearl lost the staring match. She flounced out, and you could see right there she'd reached the troublesome age, which is always worse with girls.

We waited without rioting. We cut Tansy some slack. When Pearl came back, she had a grip on the little kid who didn't want to be anywhere near here. Her bonnet hung by its strings. Her dinner pail scraped the floor. She kept setting her bare heels. "Turn me loose," she squawked. "I don't wanna, and I'm not gonna!"

Pearl pushed her toward Tansy and resumed her seat.

Tansy pulled the small girl's skirttails free of her drawers and settled her skirts for her. But it was too late. Forever more, she was known as "Little Britches."

Even unto the distant day of her wedding. Besides, come to find out her real name was Beulah.

"Who are you?" Tansy asked with an arm around her.

"I ain't sayin'," said Little Britches. "I ain't stayin'."

"Then whisper who you are in my ear before you go."

Little Britches whispered. It would turn out that she was a Bradley. They were a family who hadn't had anybody in school for some years. Little Britches was an afterthought. "I'm goin' on home now." She wiggled free of Tansy. "Pleased to meetcha."

"Well, you can go home at noon," Tansy told her. "Till then just wait up there at my desk. You can . . . help me be teacher." Tansy stuck her in the crook of her arm and climbed the rostrum to settle her in teacher's chair behind the desk. Little Britches's nose just cleared the top of it. She stared with suspicion back at us all, especially Pearl. Her eyes were still glassy with tears. Tansy was flushed from lifting her first pupil.

"Now there are seven of us," Charlie called back with the score, "and none in the privy."

"On your feet for the Pledge of Allegiance," Tansy said, remembering it. As in Miss Myrt's day, we turned to the place an American flag would hang if we had one and pledged our allegiance. Little Britches didn't, but her eyes were wide now. She was taking everything in.

The pledge lasted little longer than counting us. But we took our sweet time settling back down. Tansy pondered, then said, "Arithme—"

"Better not," Charlie called out. Though I wished he'd shut up and quit helping, he was right. Arithmetic wasn't Tansy's long suit. She knew her mathematics to the Rule of Three, but whether she could cypher into fractions, I had no idea. I knew I couldn't. Anyhow, arithmetic isn't any way to start the day.

"Spellin' School!" Charlie suggested. I'd never known that boy be so helpful. He ought to sit up there at the desk instead of Little Britches, being teacher's pet. Tansy strode to the library shelf and pulled out the blue-backed Webster speller.

Elsewhere, they called them spelling bees. We always called it Spelling School. As a school study, it was known as "orthography." It was the most important subject in the education of that time. You may not have anything to say, but you dadburn better know how to spell it.

"Divvy them up into two teams," Tansy told Little Britches.

She'd pulled her bonnet back on because she wasn't staying. She blinked out of it at us. Pointing a tiny finger, she said, "That boy at the back with the round hair."

That'd be me.

She pointed again. "That boy with the ears."

That'd be Flopears. Lloyd and Lester Kriegbaum fell in with him. That left me and Pearl and Charlie Parr on our side. Having Flopears on the opposing team made up for having to have Charlie on ours.

We pushed back the desks and squared off. Pearl didn't want to take part, but she recalled how close that pointer had come to her.

Tansy opened the Webster in front of Little Britches, who gazed down at it like a small owl. "Point to a word," Tansy told her.

"What's a word?"

Tansy showed her.

Little Britches pointed, and Tansy boomed out, "Russell Culver, *asinine*!"

"Asinine," I said. "A-double S—"

"Wrong!" Tansy grabbed up the cowbell on her desk and rang it over her head, introducing a new tradition to orthography.

"What's wrong with it?" I whined.

"Find out!" Tansy barked.

Little Britches pointed out another word.

"Lester Kriegbaum, *ascend*."

"Ascend," Lester said, "A-S-C-E-N-D. Ascend." So that put their side one ahead.

Little Britches pointed at the page. She was beginning to feel her power now.

"Pearl Nearing," Tansy said, "*asphyxiate.*" Tansy smiled slightly.

"Tell her to pick shorter words," Pearl snapped.

"*Asphyxiate.*"

"Oh, all right. Asphyxiate. A-S-F—"

The cowbell clanged.

Little Britches pushed back her bonnet, and bounced in teacher's chair. She scanned the page for another word, the longer the better.

"They don't all have to start with *A*," Tansy remarked.

"What's *A*?" Little Britches asked.

Tansy looked out at us. "Flop—Floyd Lumley, ascend the rostrum and write the letter *A* on the blackboard."

The blackboard wasn't anything as grand as slate. It was just a part of the wooden wall painted black. Flopears shambled forth. He picked up the chalk, pointed at the blackboard, and wrote a large, crooked *A*. Turning in her big chair, Little Britches gave him all her attention.

"Write, 'A is for apple,' Floyd," Tansy said, and Flopears printed:

A IS FOR APPEL

And so it went. The morning melted away as we spelled each other down and taught Little Britches her

ABC's. Tansy said we had to look up the meanings of the words too, though we'd always thought just spelling them was plenty.

"Miss Myrt didn't have us do it that-a-way!" we bleated, as we were so often to do in the days ahead.

I believe Little Britches would have settled in for the day if things had turned out better. We'd made it to *M* when she looked up from Webster and said, "I smells smoke."

An autumn haze drifted across the stifling late-August schoolroom. From out on the front step, J.W. began barking his head off. It was a regular cacophony out there. *Cacophony* was one of our *C* words. Now we all smelled smoke.

Beside me, Charlie stroked his smooth chin and suddenly jerked. He kicked his way out of the desk and sprang through the front door on his storky legs. We all followed.

As we rounded the schoolhouse, J.W. took the lead. Tansy was coming up hard from behind. The fire had a head start, and flames shot up from the back of the boys' privy. It was burning merrily in a nest of unscythed dry grass. Few things in this world smell worse than a privy on fire.

Thinking quicker than he ever did in school, Flopears was at the pump, pumping water into his hat for all he was worth. Tansy was pounding up with the pail. Everybody was running into everybody else, except for Pearl, who didn't think anything to do with the boys' privy had anything to do with her. J.W. was generally underfoot.

Me and Charlie Parr? We were pointing to the cloudless sky and ducking, saying it must have been a lightning bolt, and were we the only ones to hear that clap of thunder?

Chapter Nine

One Lucky Boy

School didn't keep the full day. Still, I was worn down to a nub by bedtime, too tuckered to sleep. As always, Lloyd was taking his half out of the middle.

"Shift over," I said. "I'm not telling you again."

"Quit your twitchin'," he said.

A sour smell of privy smoke rose off his hair, and probably mine. Apart from everything else, we were in Aunt Maud's bad books. She'd made us new feedsack shirts for the first day of school. She was handy with a needle. Lloyd had burned a hole in his shirt the size of a silver dollar. I'd burned a cuff off mine. It was all in a good cause, of course—putting out the fire before the privy could burn down to the seat.

I was just about to drift off, catching that first

glimpse of the Dakota wheat fields in the Red River valley, when Lloyd said directly into my ear, "Russell, you figure anybody found the buggy whip?"

That brought me back to life. "What buggy whip?"

"The buggy whip you and Charlie were smoking behind the privy this morning, and one of you dropped it in the weeds where it smoldered till it caught—"

"Who says we were smoking buggy whip?" I mumbled like a man talking in his sleep.

"Pearl and Flopears and Lester and—"

"All right," I mumbled. "All right."

"In fact, everybody but Little Britches, who was in the other privy. People who weren't even at school know by now. They probably know in Montezuma and Rock—"

"There's no evidence," I said. "It was a hot fire while it lasted. It burned all the undergrowth just about back to the grove."

"Russell," said Lloyd, "do you need evidence when that big a crowd catches you in the act?"

I snored then, the soft snore of first sleep.

But I was wide awake, so I noticed a random moonbeam strike the doorknob as it began to turn. Lloyd may have seen too. The door banged back. We bounced in the bed.

Tansy filled the doorway with a coal oil lamp and her hair down. In her nightdress she looked like an avenging angel. In fact, two avenging angels. She advanced on the bed, and we scrambled to the headboard, clutching our feather pillows before us.

She stood at the foot. Her lamp made fearful shadows in all the hills and hollers of the bed. It was Tansy-our-sister now, not Teacher Tansy. And there were no witnesses.

She waited while we cowered, another of our *C* words. The terrible silence undid me, and I began to babble in the night.

"We done pretty good in tamping out the fire, then raking up. Me and Char—the other boys will build up the back wall of the privy as quick as we can filch—find the lumber. I will myself personally shave enough new shingles to patch the roof . . ."

I ran out of things I was going to do as quick as I could get to them. Still, Tansy stood there. The lamplight flickered on her face.

Next to me, Lloyd was half his natural size, almost completely concealed by his pillow.

I wracked my brain for what else I better do. "And I'll get the wad out of the bell," I said. " . . . whoever done that . . ."

After a time, Tansy broke her silence. "Oh yes, you'll do all that," she said. "And more. You've had a narrow escape. You're one lucky boy. What if the fire had spread into that sugarbush grove? Do you happen to recall whose particular grove that is?"

Helpful Lloyd spoke from behind his pillow. "Aunt Fanny Hamline."

"That's right," said Tansy. "Aunt Fanny Hamline."

Tansy gave me time to picture Aunt Fanny Hamline in my mind. She was maybe the meanest living woman in Indiana now that Miss Myrt was no more.

It wasn't fair. "What about Char—"

"Did Charlie wad the bell?" Tansy spoke like lightning striking. "So if we'd had to ring it for help to fight the fire, we'd have been up a gum stump?"

"But—"

"Was it Charlie's chore to scythe the weeds around the privy in this dry weather?" Tansy pondered. "I begin to see the pattern. You muffle the bell. You leave the weeds standing. Then you set the fire."

"No, no, it wasn't nothing like—"

"But that's not your worst offense." The lamp burned lower now as my time ran out. "No. Your worst crime was to hold me up to derision."

Derision was one of our *D* words that nobody could spell. Some said it wasn't even a word, until we looked it up.

"You burned down the privy to hold me up to public derision on my first day of teaching. That is a capital offense. Men have hung for less."

I whined, "There's no evi—"

"There'll be evidence across your back end and Charlie's too. Big red welts. The smoking alone will win Charlie his stripes from Preacher Parr when I tell him and Dad about—"

"Tansy, don't," I beseeched. "We're going to make . . ."

"Restitution?" she said, though we weren't to the *R*'s yet. "You bet your sweet life you are. You'll split a winter's worth of kindling as soon as you put up the school stove. You'll be splitting kindling in your sleep. And you'll get to school every morning before me to lay the fire. You'll take down the stovepipe every two weeks like clockwork to empty the soot. You'll stack and you'll stoke and you'll take out the ashes."

"Miss Myrt always had us take them chores in turns. She—"

"And you'll have plenty of reason to miss her," Tansy said.

A whimper rose from behind Lloyd's pillow, and maybe mine.

Tansy turned at last to go. Seeming to remember something, she looked back. "And tomorrow directly school's out, you'll hitch Siren to the wagon because we're going on a little errand."

"What kind of—"

"You'll find out."

"Not me too?" Lloyd said, muffled, scared.

"No, not you, just Russell," Tansy said. "Though, Lloyd, why you can't spell *expectorate* when it's spelled just like it sounds, I cannot fathom." The lamp in her hand hissed and spat. Then Tansy was swallowed by the night. The smell of coal oil hung in the room.

I made a note in my mind to talk over our Dakota plans with Charlie. It was high time to head out. Around here things were getting too hot for us, so to speak.

In a voice small and forlorn Lloyd said, "I miss Miss Myrt. She only threatened you in daylight."

Then we must have slept.

I awoke in dread. Tansy hadn't told Dad about the privy fire because she was holding it over my head. He was bound to hear, though. And Aunt Maud too. What with the telephone and the Rural Free Delivery, there wasn't much place to hide anymore.

But when we slunk in from milking, Dad was at his place at the kitchen table with the weekly newspaper, *The Parke County Courier,* open before him.

I'd have given a lot to see a headline in it reading,

LIGHTNING STRIKES
RURAL SCHOOL PRIVY

But it wasn't to be.

"Hark at this," Dad said, and began to read:

FARM FAMILY IN NOVEL ACCIDENT
MODERN MISHAP AT COUNTY CROSSROADS

Aunt Maud had just turned out a pan of her buckshot muffins. Tansy was making our dinner. "Oh my stars, that sounds like us!" Aunt Maud said. "Who's telling our business?" She and Tansy hung over Dad as he read out the article:

> The O. C. Culver family of rural Sycamore Township was involved in an accident with an automobile last Thursday. The party was returning from a funeral when their horses drawing a Standard Wheel Company wagon shied at a near collision with a Bullet No. 2 eight-cylinder racing car driven this past winter at Daytona Beach, Florida, by Barney Oldfield.
>
> At the time of the crossroad contretemps, Eugene Hammond of the newly organized Overland Automobile Company of Terre Haute was the motorneer at the wheel of the car.
>
> The Culver family includes O. C. Culver, a prominent local citizen and practitioner of diversified farming, his handsome daughter, Miss Tansy Culver, two young sons, and Mr. Culver's sister-in-law, Miss Singleterry, who was flung some distance off the tailgate.

> Fortuitously, no injury was sustained by either the four-footed or two-footed victims of the misadventure. Eugene Hammond was able to drive the auto on to the Vigo County fairgrounds, where he demonstrated it in a time trial, finishing first.
>
> It is believed that this accident is the first such between horse-drawn vehicle and internal combustion engine in the twentieth century here in the Hoosier heartland. What lies ahead in this advanced new era? An airship colliding with a church spire? We live in miraculous times, its wonders to behold.

When Tansy saw herself called handsome in print, her hand stole up to her back hair.

Outrage etched Aunt Maud's face at anybody blaring our personal business to the listening world. "How'd they know we were coming from a funeral anyhow?"

"The way we were dressed on a Thursday," Tansy said in a far-off voice, dreamlike. "Your veil. My hat."

"Well, they got that right about me being flung a considerable distance," Aunt Maud maintained. "I was in the air long enough to see my whole life pass before me."

Dad grinned. "That young go-getter Eugene Hammond is behind this story," he said. "You can see him on every line. He hand-fed each word to the *Courier*. He'll go far, that fellow. This is better advertising for his company and himself than you can pay out money for."

Aunt Maud couldn't pull her eyes off the page. Still, her chin wagged. "I didn't expect to see my name in the paper till my obituary on the day they put me in the ground!"

"And you might not see it then," Dad remarked mildly.

Anyway, our sudden fame kept everybody's mind off my crime. I didn't feel much like one lucky boy, but at least I wasn't looking at an arson charge. Me and Lloyd attended school in our next-best shirts, sent off with a warning from Aunt Maud. This second day of Tansy's teaching went along better, and ran the full time.

Little Britches was back, on her own terms. She'd sit nowhere but at teacher's desk, and she thought she owned the Webster speller. The day unfolded as we taught her the alphabet and refreshed it for Flopears. We spelled each other down to the continual clang of the cowbell and wore the dictionary out, looking up meanings.

Our dinner pails were Karo syrup cans because of

their wire handles. We sprawled in the noonday yard and hung on the hitching rail. Pearl sat apart. Flopears had only a measly little square of hard salt-and-water corn bread in his pail that wouldn't fill a wood tick. We shared out with him, and he got a pickled peach off me. You could use the boys' privy, though the back of it was entirely gone and daylight showed through the roof.

We played our noontime games: Bug in the Gully and Old Sow Out. Tansy pinned up her skirts and played along with us to make sure nobody kicked Little Britches in the head by mistake. Charlie remarked that in a bigger school with at least nineteen pupils, you'd have two teams for real baseball, and an umpire. We looked ahead to winter and snow on the ground. Then we'd bring our rifles and hunt rabbits at noontime. But I nudged Charlie to mention privately about being up in the Dakotas by then.

At the end of the day, Tansy asked how many of us had the Monkey Ward catalog at home. Hands went up. Everybody ordered out of the catalog, and without its pages you'd have to carry corncobs to the privy.

"Look in the back of it," Tansy told us. "There's a map of the United States for giving the shipping rates. Tear out that map and bring it to school. We start geography tomorrow."

We squealed like pigs under a gate. Since somebody

had filched the school map, we'd hoped to be free of that subject. "I see no reason to study geography," Pearl said firmly, "no reason in the world."

As school days went, I'd known worse. But the threat of Tansy's errand after school hung heavy on me, whatever it was. Lloyd stayed after to shoot some marbles in the school yard with Flopears and Lester. Deciding there was a wagon ride in it for him, J.W. followed me home.

When we got there, Siren acted like she didn't want to be caught. Horses know what we don't. I had to chase her all over the lot. When I was at last backing her into the shafts, Dad called me over to the barn door. A new pile of lumber was heaped inside, five or six lengths of good, seasoned white pine planking, appearing out of nowhere.

Dad fingered his chin. "Have you any use for this?" he wondered, offhand.

"Dad," I said, "I believe I do." I'd learned some carpentry from watching him. And I had a privy that needed extensive repair. As well he seemed to know.

"You can take the lumber when you go back to pick up your sister at school," he remarked. "And you may want the ladder." So he seemed to know I'd be unwadding the bell too, whoever done that. There was no end to what Dad knew. He may have known what Tansy's errand was. But pride kept me from asking.

I loaded the wagon and talked Siren back along the Hog Scald Road, me and J.W. up on the board. We met Lloyd coming home, swinging his dinner pail. He was chewing mint and free as a bird and grinning because he wasn't me.

Chapter Ten

Stony Lonesome

Me and Tansy rode better than a mile in silence. She was Teacher Tansy in her new hat, so I felt like I ought to put up my hand to be called on. Her chin was set, and she gripped the reins herself, so she hadn't brought me along to drive. Her skirts took up most of the board. I clung to one side. Past the covered bridge over Sand Branch we turned into Stony Lonesome Road and hit the first hole hard.

It jolted me into speech. "Tansy, where in the Sam Hill are we headed?"

"I need another pupil to make eight."

"But nobody lives up Stony Lonesome Road," I pointed out. Nobody but the Tarboxes.

Dread swept me.

"Tansy, you don't mean—"

"They're a big tribe," she said, "with a bunch of kids."

"But they don't send them to school, Tansy." My heart was in my mouth. Nobody messed with Tarboxes. Tarboxes had two heads apiece. Was I along to protect Tansy? Could I look after myself?

It was slow going, veering along in dry ruts. J.W. was all over the wagon bed behind us. "Tansy, let's find us a place to turn around."

We were coming past Tarbox territory, weedy hayland and rough cropland, seen through fallen fences. Lines of old corn stubble planted in some earlier year rode the eroding rises. We smelled their home place before it came into view: the never-shoveled-out barn, the never-shifted pigpen.

Siren balked and showed unwilling. But Tansy turned her up the lane. The smell now would water your eyes. Chickens wilder than hawks flew at us. Gaunt, hopeless cows stood unmilked in the field. At least two corners of the barn needed jacking up. The well was downhill from the barn lot.

Busted implements littered the landscape. Whose implements they were was anybody's guess. The Tarboxes never knew the difference between Thine and Mine. Whatever went missing in Parke County, from a handsaw to a heifer, people said the Tarboxes got it.

"Here, there's room to turn around," I said because

we hadn't been spotted yet. A couple of people were in the privy. You could tell because it had no door on it. But they weren't looking our way.

The house was in worse shape than the barn. Tansy drew up and climbed down, and I had to follow. J.W. was on his hind legs, peering over the wagon side. The gate to the yard was off its hinges. You wanted to be real careful where you stepped. Tansy made for the house.

A rusted-out cream separator stood on the porch. It was said the Tarboxes strained their milk through an old shirt. There it was, wadded up on the peeling porch floor. A washtub webbed to the wall stood on a rickety table. In place of an oilcloth, the table was covered by a map of the world. A woman gaunt as her cattle appeared in the door. She shook off the kids clinging to her apron and stepped out.

"Well, skin me for a polecat," she said in the Hoosierest accent I ever heard. "Company! We don't get many people up this way if you don't count the sheriff."

In her hand was a length of pigtail chewing tobacco. She bit off about an ounce and returned the plug to her apron pocket.

"What can I do you for?" From behind her, eyes peered out of the gloom of the house.

"I'm the new teacher," Tansy said.

"We heard the old one kicked the bucket." Mrs. Tarbox spoke muffled. She had no teeth, and it took her some time to take control of her chaw. "But you look a good deal like Tansy Culver to me," she said. "Didn't you turn out to be a great big girl!"

Mrs. Tarbox gave Tansy the once-over. Her gaze lingered over Tansy's new hat with its bunch of artificial grapes spilling off the brim. It put several years on her. I don't suppose Mrs. Tarbox ever had a hat.

"Who's the squirt?" She meant me.

"He's one of my brothers," Tansy said. "Russell. He's along to—I like to keep an eye on him."

"I see what you mean. He looks shifty," Mrs. Tarbox said. "What's on your mind?"

"I want you to send your children to school."

"You do, do you?" Mrs. Tarbox placed a hand on her bony hip. "The ones that isn't in jail is either too young or too old."

"You're never too old to learn," Tansy said.

"Tell them that."

"If any of them are between six and sixteen," Tansy said, "the law says they go to school."

"When did they put that law through?"

"1901," Tansy said.

Mrs. Tarbox's lip curled. "Indianapolis." She shot a stream of brown tobacco juice onto the porch floor just off Tansy's left flank.

Tansy held our ground.

Mrs. Tarbox squinted aside. "Tell you what. I've got a couple inside you can have." A sound of scrambling came from inside the house. "But I'll tell you right now, they ain't housebroke."

"Are they six?"

"Not that I recollect. By the time my kids is six, they've got chores at home." She looked out over the ruined territory. "A farm don't run itself, in case you ain't heard."

Now I personally felt eyes on us from every side. Tarbox eyes from the house, the barn, up in trees. This looked like a lost cause, and I was real ready to go.

But there was still some fight in Tansy. "Don't you want them to be able to read and cypher?" She searched all the seams in Mrs. Tarbox's face.

Mrs. Tarbox clenched her jaw. "And be better than me?"

They had a staring contest then that nobody won. Finally Tansy said, "Yes."

And Mrs. Tarbox said, "Get off my land." She sounded more tired than mad.

Tansy turned, and we went. I helped her up on the board to show all the watching eyes I wasn't entirely useless.

Tansy was just turning Siren in the lot when I looked back. J.W. wasn't in the wagon bed. There was some terrier in him. That meant he dearly loved rolling in manure and decay, so Tarbox territory was the happy hunting ground for him.

I was beginning to worry when he rocketed out

from under a fence ahead of us and down the lane, barking his head off. Something moved in the ruts between here and the road. Some critter was creeping across the lane. J.W. was closing in on it with his tail high.

Tansy saw and slapped the reins on Siren's rump. J.W. snapped at the thing in the road, then jumped an easy five foot in the air. His bark turned into a terrible yowling scream.

It was a porcupine. Of all the vermin on this place, J.W. had to take out after a porcupine. Waddling at speed, it disappeared into the weeds. Still, Siren knew what it was and pulled up short. I jumped down and made a dead run for J.W. He was stretched in a rut. His screaming was already weaker, and he was pawing the air.

Before I could get to him, somebody else did. He'd vaulted the fence. Now he was bent over J.W. He was older than me, by the look of him, and with a whole lot more muscles. A Tarbox, naturally.

He glanced up. "Git a stick, three, four inches long."

"Wha—"

"Git it."

I darted off and found one and came back. He'd pulled some binder twine out of his overalls and commenced wrapping J.W.'s front and hind paws, quick and easy. He could tie a knot one-handed. He wedged the stick in J.W.'s mouth to keep it wide. A porcupine quill had lodged in the roof of J.W.'s mouth. Another quill was in his tongue, and one through an eyelid. He rolled J.W. on his back to straddle him, pulling a pair of pliers out of the loop on his overalls. They were the kind you use to fix wire fencing, though none of their fences looked fixed.

"Git a hold on his head," he told me.

He began to draw the quill out of the roof of J.W.'s mouth with the pliers. His upper arm bulged with the effort. "Them quills is barbed at the business end," he said over the sound of J.W.'s squealing. He pulled out the quill and held it up. It was the size of a darning needle. He went back for the one in J.W.'s tongue. After that, the quill through the eyelid, which was delicate work and the hardest to watch.

"Lucky," Tarbox said. "Jist three."

He untied J.W.'s legs and pulled the stick out of his mouth. When he cradled him in both hands, J.W. keened and moaned but didn't thrash.

"You got to git the quill out right now," he said, "or sometimes they'll jist stop their breathing."

We were both bent over and close. Like Charlie Parr, he could beat me to a jelly if he took a notion to. His greasy hair hung in his face, he smelled like swill, and he'd just saved my dog.

By then I felt eyes on us from closer to. Tarboxes as big as this one were standing on the far side of the fence, watching. Some had pitchforks in their hands. All their jaws worked with chaw. A fence line of tough customers.

"I'll heft him up to you," he said.

I was climbing on the board when he noticed Tansy. From up here she'd watched through Siren's ears as he'd drawn out the quills.

Handing me J.W., he said, "Tansy?" When he scooped the hair back from his eyes, I saw he must be nineteen or twenty. He wasn't as gaunt-faced as his maw, but his cheekbones stood out above the stubble.

Tansy blinked.

"Glenn Tarbox," he said. "What brings you up thisaway?"

"I wanted to talk your mother into sending some kids to school."

"Have any luck?" he said.

"No."

"Nobody has much luck with Maw," he remarked, stepping back.

"Thanks," I said, "for—"

"Git him to drink and keep him quiet," Glenn Tarbox said. "He'll swell up like a poisoned pup, but he'll be up and makin' his rounds tomorrow. He's mostly jist skeered now."

Siren jerked us through the ruts toward home. She was anxious to be out of there and back to the barn. I held J.W. like a baby. His eye was beginning to puff up, and blood gummed the corners of his mouth. He scratched at my arm so I'd hold him tighter.

"They both knew your name," I said to Tansy. "How do they know us?"

"They've got eyes and ears," she said. "They're neighbors. They're not on another planet."

"Almost, though," I said, and Tansy didn't disagree.

In a way, I felt a little bit sorry for her, working this hard to get enough pupils and still not making it. I don't think I'd ever felt sorry for her before.

"Dadrat that Tarbox woman," she said. "*And* she's having another baby."

"She is? How can you tell?"

"I'm a woman. Women know these things."

"Tansy, how come the female sex think they know more than the male sex?"

"Because we do. What's the capital of Delaware?"

"I don't know."

"Know by tomorrow," Tansy warned. "I'm the teacher, and I won't have dumb brothers."

And we jigged and jogged on home.

When we got there, she said, "Find that old quilt in the wash house and make up a bed for J.W. in your room."

"J.W. in the house?" I marveled. There was a rule against that.

"You'd just sleep in the barn with him otherwise, wouldn't you?"

"Yes," I said, and went for the quilt.

I meant to stay awake all night for J.W. But he woke me and Lloyd early the next morning, clawing at my hand dangling out of the bed. He had a big grin on his face and sported a shiner, like he'd been off on a drunk and got into a fistfight.

Me and Lloyd drilled each other out of the Monkey Ward map on the way to school. Just as well because Tansy drove us all like cattle across the United States, state by state, capital by capital, river by river. She had us studying those maps like we were Lewis looking for Clark—her and Little Britches, who was become as regular in her attendance as J.W. Pearl tapped her map and said, "I myself have no intention of visiting any of these places." But by the end of the morning, Little Britches could spell Utah, and Flopears found Indiana.

Me and Charlie spent noontime behind the boys' privy, pulling charred wood off the back of it. We sawed pine planks while the big blue horseflies a privy draws plagued us bad.

"Up in the Dakotas they don't have this insect life," I told Charlie. "They don't know what a chinch bug or a Hessian fly is up there."

"That right?" Charlie said.

We were just finding out neither one of us had brought nails when somebody stepped out of the sugar-bush grove.

It was Glenn Tarbox. I liked to jump out of my

skin. Seeing a Tarbox on their own turf was one thing. But leave it to him to stroll through Aunt Fanny Hamline's grove like it was a public right-of-way.

"Hey, Charlie," he said. He wore no shirt under his overalls, and he was muscled like a bull, tight as a tree. We had on our straw hats. You didn't go to school without a hat. Glenn was bareheaded, of course.

"Glenn," Charlie said.

"Russell," Glenn said, which surprised me. Most things came as a surprise to me in those days.

"Fire?" Glenn inquired.

"We're callin' it lightning," Charlie said.

"Smokin'?"

Charlie nodded.

"Got anything to smoke on you now?"

Charlie shook his head.

Glenn shrugged and pulled a mouthful of nails out of his overalls. A ball-peen hammer hung on one of his loops. He seemed to carry everything with him. But if he didn't, probably another Tarbox would get it. He sized up a plank and laid it against what was left of a joist. In a couple of mighty blows, he drove the first nail home. He was starting on the second when the cowbell rang.

Tansy could ring the real bell-tower bell now, but she'd fallen in love with that durn cowbell, which was hardly ever out of her hand.

Glenn looked up through his hair.

We told him it was school taking up again and turned to leave him behind. But he drove the second nail, looped his hammer, and joined us.

"You ain't comin' to school?" Charlie looked as surprised as he ever got.

"Studyin' it," Glenn said, staying right with us. J.W. was on the front step. When he saw Glenn, he shot off to tall timber, yelping. He remembered Glenn from yesterday.

Me and Charlie hung our hats, went on in, and settled at desks, Glenn following. You should have seen the look on Tansy's face. Her stated plan for that afternoon was to divvy us up among the first, second, and third readers, according to our abilities. Her and Little Britches were laying out the readers. Tansy was momentarily discommoded at the sight of Glenn. She approached. "Glenn? Are you enrolling or just passing through?"

"I'm here for the larnin'," he said, sheepish, "and the long haul."

You didn't want to get downwind of him. Tansy moved to his other side. "When I came on your place," she said, "I had in mind some of the younger—"

"You won't git any of them. They's all under Maw's thumb."

She leaned closer, and he went red through his hair. "Glenn, can you read?"

He shook his head.

"Not a word?"

No, he said, not aloud.

"Well, at least that makes us eight," Charlie announced. "We're in business."

All my hopes for shutting down Hominy Ridge School were dashed. Common sense had not prevailed, and school would keep throughout the endless year.

"That does it," I muttered to Charlie. "We're off to the Dakotas."

"Where?" Charlie said, watching Tansy's return to the rostrum, and the way she gathered her skirts.

Chapter Eleven

Trouble on the Way

I'd made up my mind that the second week of school would be my last. It took us into September, and the sands of time were running low. Anyway, Tansy had her a payload of pupils and could just mark me and Charlie absent. Once she got examined for her teacher's certificate, it'd be smooth sailing for her.

But the second week turned out to be anything but.

It began with more poetry from the Sweet Singer, who struck this time in the *Parke County Courier*.

Dad read out the article to us at breakfast Monday morning:

AUTO ACCIDENT
STIRS SWEET SINGER TO SONG

The Sweet Singer of Sycamore Township, evidently a faithful reader of these pages, was moved to poetry by last week's notice of the mishap between O. C. Culver's spring wagon and the racing car piloted by Eugene Hammond of Terre Haute.

The Singer makes his or her sentiments crystal clear in the following mellifluous lines:

Raging down the byways,
Way too fast to gauge,
Streaks the awful auto,
The terror of the age.

Burning up the rural road
At a fever pitch,
It leaves both horse and wagon
Helpless in the ditch.

The railroad was a caution
Like airships at their birth,
But the car's a living nightmare
For an unsuspecting earth.

Faster than a baseball
When you come to throw it,

Roars the awful auto
To end life as we know it.

Sincerely yours,
The Sweet Singer of
Sycamore Township

"It's not James Whitcomb Riley," Tansy remarked, "or even close."

Aunt Maud reserved judgment. Dad pushed back from the table and said, "Well, I guess I'll go practice some diversified farming." He was in the market for feeder pigs. Me and Lloyd gave Tansy a head start to school.

The boys' privy was rebuilt and newly shingled, mostly by Glenn, though Charlie wasn't a bit grateful. We still met up back there to start the day, arguing. Charlie said he didn't see how he could get away to the Dakotas until the corn was shucked. His dad preached and farmed.

"The corn won't all be shucked till October," I nagged. "What's the matter with you, Charlie? You wait for every last thing to get done, you won't go anywhere in this life."

Glenn Tarbox stepped out of the grove. He was holding up a string of dead bullfrogs, greeny-gray in the morning light. Their white legs hung far down.

"Glenn, you're going to get your fool head blowed

off if you keep cutting across Aunt Fanny Hamline's property," Charlie said. "She'd as soon shoot you as look at you. Sooner." Charlie didn't seem too grieved at the thought of Glenn being shot dead by Aunt Fanny.

"She's got her a nice pond past the grove," Glenn said, "caked with slime and full of frogs. They make real good eating. The legs does." We'd noticed he didn't bring a packed dinner in a bucket. He brought whatever he killed, and cooked it over a fire in the school yard. And enough Baldwin apples for all of us, from somewhere.

"You gig your frogs?" I inquired.

Glenn shook his head and drew a slingshot out of his back pocket. It was the polished crotch of a limb, fitted with rubber bands and a leather pouch where the rock rested. It took a dead eye to kill frogs that way, and he'd brained every one. There wasn't a mark on them, nor a drop of blood.

"I wouldn't eat one of them things if I was starved," Charlie maintained. "They's kin to snakes." But then Glenn hadn't offered him any. The cowbell clanged us inside. Glenn hung his frogs on a nail by the hats.

The mailman had been and left three big parcels. We were agog. School never got mail. Tansy set us all to work opening the boxes. Then there was oh-ing and ah-ing all around. The two biggest were poster-sized campaign portraits of the presidential contenders in this fall's election, Judge Alton B. Parker and President Theodore Roosevelt, framed.

Tansy's eyes sparked. Underneath the candidates' names was printed:

COMPLIMENTS OF
THE OVERLAND AUTOMOBILE COMPANY

SELL YOUR STEED, IT'S SPEED YOU'LL NEED

TERRE HAUTE INDIANAPOLIS

Bending to read, Tansy fingered her throat in thought. The other package was a generous pile of large notepads, and a supply of pencils, all printed with "Overland Automobile Company," also complimentary.

We'd never had pads of blank paper and pencils. We had some little cracked slates, but not one each.

"Kin we take 'em home?" wondered Flopears, who'd known few gifts.

In a faraway voice, Tansy said we could if we brought them back every day. She told us to hang the portraits over the rostrum, and Glenn had the nails. That day we pledged our allegiance directly to President Roosevelt.

We were sorted out for reading now. Little Britches, Glenn, and Charlie were in the first reader. Flopears was in the second reader by the skin of his teeth, along with Lloyd and Pearl. She'd missed the third reader by a hair and blamed Tansy. I was at the bottom of the third reader, and Lester Kriegbaum was at the top. He'd read every book in the library shelf, twice. Even *Noble Lives of Hoosier Heroes*. He needed all the powerful learning he could get to defend himself. He was so puny, you almost didn't know he was there.

We were to read to ourselves or write in our new pads while Tansy heard a group down on the recitation bench. She began with Little Britches, Glenn, and Charlie, who were a real mixed bunch. Glenn was as tall as Charlie, and Little Britches was a gnome between them. Everybody fell silent to hear her teach Glenn his ABC's.

But Little Britches's nose was full. Tansy told her not to use her sleeve and to look in teacher's desk drawer for a spare handkerchief.

Little Britches bobbed onto the rostrum and over to the desk and pulled open the drawer.

A puff adder reared up out of the drawer at her. She screamed and fell back in the chair.

A puff adder is the ugliest of all snakes. Its head, filling, swayed. I froze. I knew it wasn't poisonous, but I froze. Quicker than this telling, quicker than Charlie, Glenn was off the bench. He grabbed that snake by the neck and yanked it out of the desk. It was three foot long and real whippy. He run it back through the room, all of us ducking, and out the front door.

Tansy swept up Little Britches, who'd be crying

herself sick in another minute, and held her tight. "It didn't strike, did it?" she asked us, and we said no. We crowded around. Glancing up at me and Charlie, Tansy said, "Go get a garter snake. Quick."

"A what?"

"You heard me. A garter snake. Just a little one. Cut out."

Me and Charlie didn't need to be told twice to leave school. But a snake hunt wouldn't have been my first choice. Outside, we saw J.W. had already taken to his heels, no doubt at the sight of both Glenn and the puff adder. We ran for the ditch. Glenn came back up the road, empty-handed. "I won't kill a harmless snake," he said.

I knew it was harmless. And if you see a puff adder in the road, it'll roll over and play dead. You can pick it up on a stick, and it'll still play dead. Of course it's going to act different in a desk drawer. "Tansy wants a garter snake," I told Glenn.

I worked this ditch, and Charlie worked the other one. Glenn walked back in the field. It would have been easier in better weather. Cool slows a snake down. I personally didn't think we'd find any right away. But Charlie whooped and held one up, about two foot long, loud and unhappy.

"That's no garter snake," Glenn called out.

"I know it," Charlie yelled. "It's just the first one I come across." He flung it away.

To tell the truth, I wasn't looking with a whole heart. I don't like handling them things. Glenn slung a leg over the fence and strolled back my way. He patted his pocket, so we called Charlie off and moseyed back to school.

Little Britches's breath was still coming in sobs. Everybody else was all over the room, except for Pearl at her desk, not taking part.

Tansy tried to put Little Britches down, but she clung like a leech.

"Everybody settle in for a story." Tansy walked over to the picture of Theodore Roosevelt, with Little Britches hitched up on her hip.

"Who knows where the President lives?"

"Indianapolis!" Flopears sang out. He was chockful of geography, most of it wrong, and always willing to share.

"Washington, D.C.," Tansy said, "in the White House." Little Britches had buried her face in Tansy's shirtwaist.

"Does he have any kids?" Tansy asked.

Durned if we knew.

"He does," Tansy said. "Four boys and two girls. This is the First Family of America. What are their names?"

Search us.

"Theodore, Junior," Tansy said. "Kermit, Ethel, Archibald, and Quentin.

"And Alice is the oldest. She is the President's daughter by his first marriage." Little Britches held on. We all listened.

"The Roosevelts have turned the White House into a regular menagerie." Which was one of our *M* words. "Quentin brought his Shetland pony, named Algonquin, up in the elevator for a visit to Archie's room when Archie was in bed with diphtheria. Kermit has a pet kangaroo rat who likes sugar in a cube. And they've got a parrot and a blue macaw."

Where Tansy came up with her information we didn't know. But it was fairly interesting. "Guess what Alice's pet is."

"A kitty," Little Britches said against the shirtwaist.

"No," Tansy said, "Alice's favorite pet is a little green garter snake that lives in her purse."

"No," Little Britches said. "Not a doggone snake."

"Yes," Tansy said. "I'm the teacher. Believe it." She put her other hand out and snapped a finger at Glenn. He reached into his pocket. You could have heard a pin drop. We were all as silent as Sunday afternoon.

Glenn handed over a skinny little more-or-less green garter snake, ten or so inches long. We watched it spill out of his hand into Tansy's. It wrapped once around her wrist and coiled in her palm. Its eyes were like little diamond chips.

"Say listen, I think Alice's pet garter snake has come to pay us a visit," Tansy said.

"Better not." Little Britches spoke muffled against Tansy's bosom.

"Why, here it is."

Now even Pearl stood at her desk, staring transfixed. Little Britches chanced a quick glance. "If that thing's somebody's pet," she said, "what's its name?"

"Eutaenia sirtalis," Tansy said without skipping a beat. "All garter snakes have the same name."

She must have picked up more learning at high school than we'd figured.

The garter snake was content in the warm hollow of Tansy's hand. Little Britches chanced another glance. She just touched the tail hanging down from Tansy's wrist.

"Shall we keep her?" Little Britches wondered.

"Alice wants her home," Tansy said. "We'll turn her loose so she can get going."

Little Britches needed another hug. But then she slid down Tansy's skirts and bobbed back to the recitation bench. Tansy had swapped one snake for another in Little Britches's mind. It must have worked, because she looked to be recovered. Now she was pulling Glenn and Charlie down on the bench, to say, "Repeat after me,

"**A** is for the animals who keep us alive,
B is for the busy bee, buzzing round the hive."

"Russell Culver," Tansy commanded, "see me outside." She always called me Russell Culver at school, like we weren't kin. Out on the front step, she whispered, "Get that thing off me, quick, and fling it in the ditch." She was flushed, but underneath that, paler than death. "I can't stand a snake." I unwound it, and it slithered off.

"Tansy, does Alice Roosevelt really carry a pet snake around in her purse?" I asked.

"Of course she does," Tansy snapped, "as you'd know if you ever read anything. Sometimes you act like you haven't been born." She was still real jumpy about having that snake around her wrist.

To calm her down, I said, "You done some pretty quick thinking in there. I'll give you credit."

"Never mind about that," she said. "Not one word of this snake business to Dad, you hear me? I have only myself to blame. When I got to school this morning, the front door lock was broken. I should have seen trouble on the way."

Sure enough, the front door was jimmied and splintered. What I wanted to know was, who broke in with a sack full of puff adder? Whose hands shook out that sack into the desk drawer? How many hands?

"Remember, not a peep to Dad and certainly not to Aunt Maud," Tansy said, "or else. I can handle this. I have to. I'm the teacher. And put a lid on Lloyd. He babbles like a brook. Now, back inside. You and Lester are reciting next."

And that was that. From out of the schoolroom warbled Little Britches's piping voice:

"**C** is for the cattle, lowing in the sheds,
D is for the daffodils, nodding in their beds."

Then Charlie's baritone and Glenn's bass, working the same territory.

No power on earth would keep a lid on Lloyd. At supper that night, he announced, "Tansy's got a secret."

She shot him a deeply dangerous look.

"Are we going to have to hear what it is?" Dad inquired.

"She's got her an S-W-double E-T-H-E-A-R-T, as we say in Spelling School."

Tansy eased off, a little.

"And his initials are E.H., for Eugene Hammond," Lloyd informed us. "He's sending us stuff at school to get on her good side."

It dawned on me that's where Tansy's new hat with the grapes came from. But me and Dad had the sense to keep quiet.

Not Aunt Maud. "Well, why wouldn't she have a whole bunch of swains and sweethearts lined up for her all the way back to the windpump?" Aunt Maud demanded. "Good-lookin' girl like that!"

Tansy preened slightly, a sight in itself.

Me and Lloyd blinked. That was a new one on us. Could it be that Tansy was a good-looking girl and we hadn't noticed because she was our sister? We gaped. And our teacher? We wondered.

That night in bed, Lloyd said, straight in my ear, "Russell, you asleep?"

"Yes," I said, "but if I wasn't I'd ask you a question."

"What?"

"If you sass Tansy at the supper table, aren't you worried she'll take it out of you at school?"

Silence from the middle of the bed. It had never crossed his mind. Then he said, "Russell, I think she's turning out to be not too bad a teacher."

"Well, learn plenty," I told him, "and tell me all about it when and if I get back." Then I slipped into sleep to the distant sound of steam engines threshing Dakota wheat.

Chapter Twelve

Another Old Gal in the Ditch

Seemed like Tansy was never satisfied. If it wasn't orthography, it was looking up meanings. If it wasn't looking up meanings, it was geography. Then history, then I don't know what. Now it was numbers.

"Six is to eight as twelve is to . . ." That kind of thing, which was irritating to me. Tansy had an arithmetic book, *The Western Calculator,* from the high school. She pored over it at home in the evenings, keeping a day ahead of us. At this rate we'd be looking at multiplication tables before the month was out.

The weather was still hotter than hinges, with only a glint of goldenrod. Me and Lloyd slumped to school through clouds of midges. But already Aunt Maud was introducing winterish hot oatmeal into our breakfasts. And her hot oatmeal tasted like pullet mash.

Attendance at school was good, here before harvest. I thought every day would be Glenn's last, but he was still Johnny-on-the-spot. And Tansy kept coming up with new ideas never heard of in schoolteaching. Seemed to me, if she'd been trained right as a teacher, she'd stick to the rules more. But she combined Spelling School with geography and split us into teams to name all forty-five state capitals *and* the territorial capitals *and* spell them. So we started off Thursday morning spelling each other down. And you couldn't look at your map. You had to know, which we said wasn't fair. I dreaded what she was saving up for me. And what about Glenn, who couldn't spell his own name, let alone a capital city? As things turned out, it never came to that.

"Pearl Nearing," Tansy rang out. "Iowa."

Pearl got an easy one and sneered. "The capital of Iowa," she said, "happens to be Des Moines. Capital D-E, capital M—"

Clang went the cowbell. Down went Pearl.

"Russell Culver." Tansy smiled slightly. "Florida."

I sighed. "The capital of Florida is Tampa. Capital T-A—"

"No, it ain't!" said several. Suddenly everybody was an expert.

"It's Tallahassee," piped Little Britches.

"I know it," I whined, "but I can spell Tampa."

Tansy reached for the cowbell to give me a double

clang when we all heard a sudden sound from outside: a splintering of wood and a screech, then a howl from J.W. All louder than the crack of doom.

What now? Tansy spoke under her breath. We all crowded outside. J.W. was cowering against the school with one paw up. Looked like he'd had a nasty shock.

The plank across the ditch had split under the weight of a real big, real old lady. Her bonnet was askew, and she was flat on her back, waving a cane. My land, she was enormous. She'd make Tansy look like Little Britches. She was down at the bottom of the ditch, but her bosom was level with the road.

And mad? As a hornet. You couldn't hardly follow her. But it seemed to be, "Somebody'll pay for this and pay through the nose," and "If I ever get out of this ditch, there are some who'll wish to heaven I hadn't." Things like that. She was spitting like a bobcat on a chain.

Tansy pushed through us and looked in the ditch. "Oh no," she said. "Aunt Fanny Hamline."

I thought we'd need a block and tackle to lift her. But getting Aunt Fanny Hamline out of the ditch became one of Tansy's most famous days of teaching. It was a lesson in engineering too. It should have been studied at Purdue University.

We needed rope and sent Lester as the smallest boy up the bell rope in the tower. Being puny paid off, and up he swarmed in his Buster Brown collar with a knife in his teeth. He whittled away at the rope above him. And when it snapped, we were in a bunch below to catch him and the rope.

Getting it under Aunt Fanny took longer. Squaring off in the same teams as state capital Spelling School, we started above her bonnet and slipped the rope under, sawing back and forth to get it down to the middle of her. Not to her waist. She didn't have a waist. It was heavy work even with all hands at it. The hardest part was staying out of range of her cane.

And noisy? "You brats is rubbing all the skin off my backbone," and "I'll have the law on ever' one of you, individually," and "You can run, but you cain't hide," and "I know where you live." Things like that.

Once her cane swung too near Glenn. He grabbed it out of the air and flung it in the road, and that slowed her down some.

When we got the rope centered, our problems began. She wouldn't sit up, and we couldn't budge her flat. We heaved and we hoed and we got nowhere. If one team heaved while the other was hoing, she'd begin to revolve. If somehow we happened to flip her over on her front, she could drown in the ditch. There was always some standing water in the ditch, even in dry weather. This would quiet her, but then she'd come back to haunt us. We were getting right down to the end of our rope, so to speak.

Just then the mailman, Mr. George Keating, making his regular rounds, drew up. We seemed to come as a surprise to him. Aunt Fanny stretched out full-length and hollering from the ditch. All eight of us pulling at her with the bell rope, like tug-of-war. The cowbell still in Tansy's fist.

Mr. Keating ran a hand around the back of his neck, saying, "And I thought I'd seen everything." If it hadn't been for the mailman, Aunt Fanny would still be in the ditch. We decided to tie both ends of the bell rope to the back of his mail wagon. Though Aunt Fanny Hamline outweighed his horse, with all eight of us and Tansy pushing the wagon and pulling on the rope and the horse straining and pawing the road, we showed some progress.

Aunt Fanny began to skid on wet reeds. Her bosom moved like hedgehogs just even with the road. Then she was skidding sitting up, her bonnet still askew. Then she was on her feet, tramping the ditch at a brisk pace and trying to work out of the rope around her before the horse broke into a trot.

Even on her feet, it was no Sunday-school picnic lifting her out of the ditch. But four of us behind and four of us before, and finally Aunt Fanny staggered up onto solid ground. There wasn't a whole lot left to the back of her skirts, and she was drenched with ditch water all up that side. We retrieved the rope, and Mr. George Keating went on his way, no doubt to spread the word. Somebody found her cane. J.W. slunk off in search of quiet.

Aunt Fanny herself was nearly winded. It had been a workout for a woman of her years and size. Her breath came in wheezes. But she returned to life pretty quick. Without invitation, she stomped into the schoolhouse, filling it up. We followed.

Some of us had never set eyes on her. She'd lived in her house in the grove since right after the ark came ashore. And she was but seldom seen.

It was said that she never left her place for fear somebody would charge her money for something. She was so tight, they said, that she'd sit out under a tree on a hot day to save the shade on her porch. Cheap? She'd skin a louse for its hide and tallow.

"What's this place supposed to be?" Aunt Fanny pointed her cane in various directions.

"This is a public schoolhouse," said Tansy, "as you know."

"Well, it don't look anything like one to me. Where's the American flag?"

"The taxpayers haven't seen fit to provide one," Tansy said. "I take it you're a taxpayer."

Aunt Fanny jumped on that. "Girl, I'm the biggest taxpayer in Sycamore Township and maybe Parke County, and I get the least for my money. Who are you supposed to be?"

"I'm the teacher here," Tansy said.

"Piffle," said Aunt Fanny. "Myrt Arbuckle was the little end of nothin' whittled down to a fine point, but you ain't even—"

"Don't talk me down in front of my pupils," Tansy warned.

"Who's to stop me?"

"I am." Tansy held her ground, and Aunt Fanny faltered. We gaped. It was hard to see Tansy around her. There were ferns plastered to Aunt Fanny's whole backside. And a tuft of dark fur. Minks like wet ditches. We wondered if she'd flattened one.

"State your business," Tansy said, pretty pert. "I have teaching to do and knowledge to impart."

"Well, impart this to your so-called pupils. Tell 'em to keep off my property. One or more is trespassin' and stealin' from me." Aunt Fanny seemed to address the bracket that used to hold the map. Her eyesight wasn't up to snuff, and she naturally wouldn't pay for spectacles. "I don't see like I did, but they's bound to be your bunch. *And* they's giggin' my frogs."

Tansy looked around her at us. "Anybody here gigging Aunt Fanny's frogs? Pearl, have you been gigging Aunt Fanny's frogs?"

Since a gig is a pole five foot long with a metal frog-sticker on the end of it, you couldn't really picture Pearl with one in her hand. Neither could Pearl. "Certainly not! I have never laid a finger on a frog. The idea! None of this has anything to do with me." She patted the enormous bow on the back of her head.

Aunt Fanny looked thunder-struck. "Who's that stuck-up little—"

"Fl—Floyd Lumley," Tansy called out around her, "have you been gigging Aunt Fanny's frogs?"

"No, Miss Myrt!" Flopears sang out.

Aunt Fanny's old pink-rimmed eyes popped. "Well, he ain't the sharpest tool in the shed, is he?" she observed.

We saw what Tansy was up to. She was wearing down Aunt Fanny one so-called pupil at a time. Lucky there was no string of frogs hanging out by the hats this particular morning. Though of course they wouldn't have been gigged. They'd have been brained by a slingshot.

Aunt Fanny's half-blind gaze swept teacher's desk where Little Britches and a Baldwin apple were. She didn't see either. Glenn had brought apples for all this morning, we didn't know where from.

"I've got apples comin' on from the trees up by my house," Aunt Fanny imparted to us, "and I have ever' one of them apples counted. Believe it."

We did.

"And I'll tell you all something else for free." She rapped her cane on the floor. "I may be blinder than any bat, but I got me a government-issue rifle. It was the one my husband, Mr. Hamline, carried when he fought with Captain Lilly's Eighteenth Indiana Light Artillery at Chicamauga."

Her husband? Aunt Fanny had been married? Lloyd went pale as this page.

"And I can lock and load while you're lookin' for your feet. If you can outrun a bullet, come see me. Otherwise, keep off my place!"

She turned to go, and her skirts made a rusty sound. We fell back, and Charlie came in the door. We'd been too occupied to miss him. In his big hands were the two halves of the plank across the ditch.

"Somebody's sawed this plank half through," he announced.

We blinked, and some of us remembered the snake in the drawer. Charlie remembered. Except for Glenn, who came through the grove, we'd all crossed the plank this morning. Tansy too, and she's no wood nymph, as I've mentioned. But Aunt Fanny must have been the last straw, so to speak.

"And now you're tryin' to kill me," she said, "or cripple me up for life." Out she went, but turned back at the door. She pointed an old bent finger, sighted down it, and cocked a thumb. "Jist try me," she said. Then she was gone, more or less in a puff of smoke.

* * *

That was also the day I finally talked Charlie into heading off for the Dakotas no later than Saturday night. I pulled out all my arguments in favor of this enterprise.

At last Charlie seemed to stir at the salary of seventeen dollars a week for the threshing season, and keep. We'd get there for free, as long as the freight trains ran. I liked the sound of riding the rods, however you did that. But it was the seventeen dollars that seemed to win Charlie.

Still, it was harder than usual to get him to concentrate. The sawed plank and the puff adder preyed on his mind. I told him to put the whole business behind him, and school too.

"All right," he said at long last. "I'm tired of hearin' about it. Saturday night."

A thrill shot through me with some fear in it. Now that Charlie had caved in made it real. We'd have to sneak off without good-byes. Charlie was of legal age to quit school, but I wasn't, quite. Anyway, sneaking off was part of the deal. We'd slip out of our houses after everybody was in bed, meet up, and make for Montezuma for the Monon freight train that went through late. Up in the Chicago yards, we'd find us a train of the Great Northern Line. I knew it by heart. Boys from these parts went up every year.

"Remember, wear your winter suit under your

overalls," I told Charlie. I spelled it out for him. You had to. "You don't want to carry anything in your hands. Bring eats in your pockets. You got all this?"

He claimed he did, so finally we were on our way to the big skies of the Dakotas and to the Red River valley, the American Nile. What could stop us now?

Chapter Thirteen

The Only Really Perfect Thing in the World

That Friday morning Mr. George Keating, the mailman, had another parcel for school, a big one. He delivered it straight into the classroom and stayed on to see what was in it.

We were doing numbers, so everybody was ready to stop, including Tansy. We unwrapped it and saved the string. Then we looked down into the box at the top of a human head. When we got it out, it was a plaster bust of The Great Emancipator, President Abraham Lincoln, finished like bronze. We oh-ed and ah-ed and read out the inscription on the pedestal:

IF THERE'D BEEN MOTORCARS,
HE'D HAVE DRIVEN ONE OF OURS

COMPLIMENTS OF
THE OVERLAND AUTOMOBILE COMPANY
TERRE HAUTE—INDIANAPOLIS

I glanced at Tansy standing back. She was a shade pinker.

The bust of President Lincoln would bring great dignity to our library shelf. But when we got it out of the box, something else was wedged in the bottom. Pearl grabbed for it. She unwrapped it and shrugged. It was just a baseball, which had nothing to do with her.

Glenn had it then, and held it up. It was snow white with red stitching. Regulation.

Our hearts turned over. We'd never been this close to a real baseball. Our only baseballs were the ones we made, ourselves, pig leather stuffed with horsehair and stitched at home. They were never round. They neither bounced nor rolled. And they never lasted.

The ball, the only really perfect thing in the world, rested in Glenn's cupped palm. Lester gazed up at it in awe. Flopears came close to comprehending. There was a lump in Lloyd's throat. I saw through a blur of tears. The ball was naturally stamped: "Compliments of the Overland Automobile Company."

"I suppose this means immediate recess," Tansy said.

Mr. George Keating stayed on to play a round of catch with us. Pearl sat up on the hitching rail, retying her hair bow. But the rest of us took part. Tansy too, to see that we'd roll the ball to Little Britches for her turn. Playing catch was enough for now. We couldn't play a real ball game, and we hadn't gotten to Four-Cornered Cat yet. For now it was enough to feel that baseball, still white and perfect, slide into your hand like it was coming home, to see the arc of it against the dark blue sky. To feel the throw in your shoulder.

These were perfect moments, and they passed.

Though on in years, Mr. Keating had a stylish windup and follow-through. But he remembered he had mail to deliver and went on his way. We'd pushed recess to its limits. As quick as Tansy got the ball, she'd call time and lead us back to learning.

So Charlie and Glenn set up a back-and-forth between themselves. We didn't have ball gloves, so you heard the smack of the ball in the heel of the hand. It got louder. The ball was a blur between them now. Charlie was redder in the face. Glenn's upper arm strained and glistened.

Then it all went wrong, which is the way it was heading all along. Glenn threw a little wild and caught Charlie's guard down. The ball glanced off his right temple, popped up, and bounced off the schoolhouse wall behind him.

Charlie swayed, stunned. Then he took out after Glenn, springing like a panther across the yard. Dust rose behind him. Glenn had just time to make that come-and-get-me gesture with both hands. Then they were squaring off, but not throwing punches yet. You fought fairer in those days. You not only had to keep your chin down, you had your good name to think about.

Tansy grabbed up Little Britches to enfold her, but that seemed all she could think to do.

Charlie swung. He was longer in the arm, and his fist connected with Glenn's stubbled jaw.

"That's for the puff adder," Charlie yelled out. They were nose to nose now.

"You crazy fool," Glenn growled. "What are you talkin' about?"

"And that's for the plank—"

But Glenn brought a left hook out of nowhere. It laid Charlie's nose sideways, though he was still standing.

"Why would I do them things?" Glenn hollered at him.

"Why?" Charlie worked around to swing again. "To make yourself the big hero."

"Whose big hero?" Glenn ducked and danced.

"Tansy's hero."

The world stopped dead to listen. Even Pearl. Tansy turned Little Britches's face to her skirts.

Glenn had stuck the puff adder in the drawer and sawed the plank to be Tansy's hero? Why did he want to—

"You didn't figure the plank would hold till Aunt

Fanny got on it." The blood gushed from Charlie's nose. "You lurked around, hopin' to lift Tansy out of the ditch just like you grabbed the snake out of the drawer, *where you put it.* Big hero!" They'd both forgotten to fight. Charlie was up in Glenn's face. "Tarbox trash."

That did it. Glenn sprang. He was shorter in the arm, but pure gristle. Down they went, rolling in the dirt, throwing punches like a piston engine gone haywire. Dust whipped into a fog. Charlie and Glenn were a frenzy of flailing elbows and kicking heels and the sounds of smacking.

The rest of us stood there, up on our hind trotters, watching. Though it was none of my put-in, I edged around to Tansy. "They can't keep this up," I said, but they did, seemed like forever. At last they both fell back, not a punch left in either one of them.

Little Britches was scared and crying. Tansy set her aside and walked over to the two sprawling figures and gave them both good, swift kicks.

"Get over to the pump, the pair of you," she said, "and put your heads under it."

But they couldn't move for the moment.

"Either that," Tansy's voice spiraled up, "or I'll . . . turn you in to Aunt Fanny and tell her you're both stealing from her."

Still they stayed put, though when one sat up, the other one did too.

"You're neither one heroes to me," Tansy said while we all listened. "Far from it, you lummoxes. You're nothing in this world but . . . half-witted . . . half-wild . . . Hoosier . . . hicks."

Tragedy struck then. Tears spilled and streamed down Tansy's face, though she threw back her head to stem their flow. The sobs came then, faster than she could swallow. A teacher dares not cry, not a real teacher. Tansy looked in her hands for the cowbell, but it wasn't there. "Go on," she said in a broken voice. "Clean yourselves up."

Charlie limped to his feet, but said, "I ain't goin' nowhere." His shirtfront was red with blood. He held up a hand swelling already. You could tell from here that he'd broken it. He'd broken his hand on a rock-hard Tarbox jaw.

He looked up at me through a closing eye and repeated himself. "I ain't goin' nowhere."

And there was but one thing I understood. Me and Charlie weren't lighting out for the Dakotas after all. All my dreams were dust, and maybe Tansy's too.

We cut hay all that Saturday, me and Dad. I'd meant to give him a good day's work anyway, when I thought it would be my last. So that part was the same.

I couldn't handle the Dakotas on my own, and I cursed a fate that knocked out Charlie at just the wrong moment. Was this the kind of luck I had ahead of me from here on? I was low in my mind and supposed Dad didn't notice.

Lloyd spent the day down at the barn. He was raising a calf by hand on skim milk. It was the kind of foolish, farmerish enterprise that appealed to him. I wouldn't have had the patience.

He was coaching the calf to drink from a pail. And a calf is dumber than a pig. The calf would get the pail wallering around on the ground and spill half the milk out. Then it'd get its nose in too far and start drowning. Then it'd throw its head and snort milk in every direction and all over Lloyd.

Why anybody would want a day like that, I couldn't tell you. But Dad let Lloyd off to have it.

The hay we were cutting was to feed the cattle through the winter when they couldn't get out to pasture. Dad thought we might get three cuttings out of the first bottomlands. He always knew when to cut the hay when it had the most milk in it, as we put it in those days.

Little was said at supper. Tansy and Aunt Maud had been canning preserves out of the last of the green zebra tomatoes. That smell hung heavy in the kitchen air. Tansy looked drawn and grim, brought close to hopeless about her teaching. I was trapped for life and never would get off the place. For once, Lloyd didn't have anything to say. If he was glad he wouldn't lose me to the Dakotas, he didn't mention it.

I never had thought he looked up to me like he should.

Afterward, Dad told me to get the ladder, and we'd ride down to school to run the rope back up the bell tower. He'd cut and planed a new plank for over the ditch too.

There was only one minor mystery about the evening, as far as I could see. When they were clearing the table, Aunt Maud sent Tansy upstairs to "change." Though whether Tansy was to change her mind or her dress, Aunt Maud didn't say.

Lloyd stayed down at the barn to have a talk with his calf. Me and Dad and J.W. headed off along the road to school behind Stentor, into the sunset. We took the buggy since it was only the three of us, and tied the ladder on the side.

We weren't long about our schoolhouse business. Dad never wasted time with extra talk. When we climbed back up in the buggy, we headed on down the Hog Scald Road, away from home. The light was fading. "Dad, are we going to look at a cow?"

He'd buy half-starved cattle off patch farmers, feed them out, and sell them on. But this was a peculiar time of day for it.

Dad said he thought we'd give Stentor a stretch and run on into Montezuma.

Montezuma? An hour each way, in the dark? But I didn't say anything. J.W. hunkered in my lap and snapped at lightning bugs. The thick dust of the road cushioned the buggy wheels. I fell into a daze. This is the road I'd meant to walk, later tonight, meeting up with Charlie. We'd have worn our winter suits under our overalls, with eats in our pockets. We'd have lit out.

I might have dozed off, because now you could see the lights of Montezuma as we came down the hill into it, and the black Wabash River beyond. I couldn't figure why we were here. Nothing would be open, and we didn't know anybody.

Stentor shied at the city lights and threw his tail. We thundered across a section of wood-block paving in front of the depot. Dad turned down a darker street that crossed the Monon tracks. A line of boxcars on a siding cast a long shadow. Down that way, campfires flickered, putting me in mind of going to the crick with Lloyd, and Charlie.

You could begin to see the shapes of human heads between here and the flames. We pulled up a little short of them. They were tramps, waiting for the freight that went through north in the middle of the night. Their bundles were piled around. They were cooking their mulligan over the fires. They may have been Dakota-bound.

One of them broke from the others and started for us. He was drunk, weaving in half circles, swinging a bottle. His other hand was out, wanting something from us. A growl rumbled low in J.W.'s throat. Dad reached for the whip socket, and the tramp turned back to the fire.

Figures, rough customers, slouched in the boxcar doors, smoking. Pinpoints of orange light glowed in their cupped hands. We sat on a while longer, just out of the firelight. It began to come to me why we were here. Dad knew, somehow. He knew this was the night I'd meant to light out, and he was showing me where I'd have gone. It wasn't like I'd pictured it, nor anywhere I wanted to be. But I'd have had Charlie along to—

"Charlie wasn't ever coming," said Dad, who could evidently read minds.

"But, Dad, we had us a plan from way back, to—"

"Son, I think it was all your plan. Charlie had him a different one. I believe he's pursuing it right now back at our house. He's busier than a one-armed cornshucker, trying to get back into Tansy's good graces after that dustup in the school yard. And who do you think it was gave her the cowbell, the first day of school?"

"You? Playing fair?"

"Charlie. Playing for himself," Dad said. "And broken hand or no broken hand, he's not about to leave a clear field for Glenn Tarbox."

"Glenn Tarbox? What—"

"Those boys are butting heads over Tansy."

Tansy? My head swam. "But, Dad, why?"

Dad seemed to smile. "Son, if I have to explain that to you, we'll be here till morning."

Dad turned Stentor away from the worrisome scene in the railroad yard. We headed on back the way we'd come, shoulder to shoulder in the crickety night. The schoolhouse bell tower was a shape against the starry sky before I knew where we were. As we stopped to get the ladder, I said, "Dad, I wouldn't have lived up all my wages, in the Dakotas. I'd have sent money back."

And after a little while, he said, "I'd sooner have you home."

Part III

The Fall of the Year

✯ ✯ ✯

Chapter Fourteen

One Serious Suitor

From the *Parke County Courier,* Rockville:

ODE TO AUTUMN

The evenings now is drawing in;
They's a ring around the moon;
The geese is passing overhead
Morning, night, and noon.

The leaves is flowing down the crick
Like cider from the press,
And when the first frost's coming
Is anybody's guess.

With peaches yet to pickle
And the weather getting fickle,
With the hogs back in their pens
And the Baldwins in their bins,
School bells sound across these lands,
And at last the kids is off our hands.

Praise the Lord!

Sincerely,
The Sweet Singer of
Sycamore Township

Forces largely unseen kept me from the Dakotas.

It was years before I got up there. Then it was on a motoring trip me and my wife took to the Black Hills in 1926, the first year they made the Pontiac. By then the world was a different place. The hard roads were coming through, and you could drive most of the way from Montezuma, Indiana, to Sioux Falls, South Dakota, on slab. But that was far in the invisible future. If there's one thing you can't see at the age of fifteen, it's ahead.

Me and Lloyd kicked along in the dust of the road every school morning through countryside rusting with autumn. The ground was tufted with purple ironweed. Flea beetles had chewed the hedge leaves to gauze. I made an early start to split kindling against the day we put up the school stove.

I went off in the crisping mornings, resigned. Relieved. Cushioned by a father's quiet love. Directed by a sister's bullet-tipped pointer.

She'd rallied and was back in charge at school now, and then some. Charlie's big mitt was three times its size in a bandage that stayed on right up to Thanksgiving. This called a truce between him and Glenn Tarbox. I watched them like a hawk to see if Dad's theory held water and they were both sweet on Tansy. But I couldn't tell much, except that Glenn had perfect attendance, and somebody had cut his hair.

The last of the peaches were the Yellow Crawfords, ripe in October. Glenn brought a peck basket of them, from somewhere, and left it on Tansy's desk.

Him and Charlie gave each other a wide berth whenever they weren't down on the recitation bench. Then, Little Britches sat between them. Under her direction, the three of them were rounding third base on the alphabet:

> "**V** is for the violet, in the timber's shade;
> **W** is for willow, weeping in the glade."

Tansy had us on an even keel now. But she hid the regulation baseball, to keep the peace.

She only had to whup one of us all fall. Sadly, it was me. Or as she'd put it, Russell Culver. It all came to pass because of Elocution.

Elocution was the subject we always had Friday. That was when we held a program of our accomplishments. You'd recite or sing a song or work an arithmetic problem on the board—anything to show how you could speak up in public. You couldn't be tongue-tied nor catch a case of lockjaw, or Tansy would give you an F. She was quick with her F's.

On one of the Fridays, Little Britches said she'd learned a poem by heart and wanted to give it as her party piece for Elocution. So Tansy let her, and we all settled back to listen as Little Britches sashayed to the center of the rostrum, gathered her hands, and elocuted in a high voice that rang like a little bell:

Adder in the desk drawer,
Aunt Fanny in the ditch;
Life here at Hominy Ridge
Surely is a—

With an almighty thwack, Tansy brought her pointer down on the desk. Little Britches jumped.

"Who taught you that so-called verse?"

Little Britches pointed me out and said, "Russell Culver."

So I got a sound whupping from a switch I had to cut myself. And I'll tell you something else. Nobody felt a bit sorry for me. Not even Little Britches, who'd been so quick to turn me in.

* * *

Resigned though I was to learning and knowledge, I'd hoped Dad would let us lay out of school for the corn shucking. Even Lloyd was big enough now to pull his weight. It wasn't to be. We shucked before and after school, but never during. When the corn was dry enough to crib, we hitched up Siren and Stentor to the wagon and had them in the field by daylight. There was frost on the stalks now.

Siren and Stentor were trained for the work, so they knew to draw the wagon in a straight line, knocking a corn row down. We'd come along behind on foot to shuck the ears. I had a chain-link finger stall for ripping open the shucks. I forget what Lloyd had. Dad used a hand-whittled peg fixed to a leather strap around his wrist. He could shuck very nearly a hundred bushel a day.

We built up one side of the wagon with twelve-inch widths of lumber we called bang boards. The corn ears we flung in the wagon would bounce off the boards to fill the bed.

It was a workout. After my fingers thawed, I'd have slept through the school day if I'd dared. Charlie was bright as a button because his hand kept him out of the field. Who knew what chores Glenn did at home? But he had him a new shirt with buttons that matched, and it didn't look handed down.

I never will forget one evening when we were coming back from the field, me and Dad and Lloyd. It was Indian summer when there's warmth again in the setting sun. We'd shoveled the corn ears into the crib. Now we were walking up from the lot when we heard music, of all things.

It stopped us cold. We'd never heard music hanging like haze over the blue evening. I recalled the calliope on the Case Special, trilling down the track. But we were miles from the railroad, and this was a full orchestra, with violins. Dad himself looked like he didn't know where he was.

Around the front of the house, an automobile was drawn up. It wasn't the Bullet No. 2 racer. It had a roof with roll-down side curtains. Right-hand drive. But we naturally thought of Eugene Hammond. Besides, he was the kind of man who could muster music out of thin air.

When the front porch came into view, we saw an Edison Victrola with a flared horn lacquered and gilded. Working its crank was Tansy. But what turned my world upside down was this. Eugene Hammond was on the porch, in a windowpane plaid suit and his cap on backward with goggles pushed up. With a woman in his arms.

It was Aunt Maud.

They were waltzing to the strains of "Build Me a Bower of Moonbeams." Aunt Maud dancing on the front porch with Eugene Hammond to blaring music where the neighbors could see? Did he know she smoked a cob pipe?

Her face was tucked into his shoulder, and her back hair was coming unpinned as they swooped from railing to railing. If she threw a shoe, we'd have to shoot her. Tansy looked on from the crank, smiling privately.

Lloyd was shocked senseless. I didn't know whether to look or look away. Seemed like Eugene Hammond had gone too far this time. And he was hanging on around these parts like a summer cold.

"Dad," I said, low, "what does it mean?"

"It means he's stepping up his pace. Now he's courting the whole family," Dad remarked. "He's one serious suitor, and he's proving it this minute."

"Dad," I breathed, "what had we better do?"

"Son, I don't know." Dad stifled a smile. "Do you think we ought to take steps?"

We butchered two or three Saturdays after that. By then a raw wind rattled the empty corn shocks, and we were wearing shoes to school.

Hallowe'en had fizzled out, what with Charlie's hand keeping us from mischief. Lloyd and Flopears and Lester went out one night and stuffed a given amount of road apples into people's mailboxes. But that was about the size of it. Everybody naturally steered clear of Aunt Fanny Hamline's place. We weren't as dumb as we looked.

Butchering day was as big as Thanksgiving to us. Our neighbors came to help and for the sociability of the thing. Aunt Maud had come down the road in the darkest reaches of the night, behind her glowing pipe. Her and Tansy bustled by lamplight in the kitchen because there was a world of sausage and scrapple to be made, and breakfast, and a noon dinner for the multitude. Me and Lloyd had a fire going under the big barrel out in the lot. It was cold as charity that black morning of butchering day.

And on this particular occasion, Dad had invited Eugene Hammond to take part.

I had the idea Dad had invited him to the butchering to call his bluff and show him up. Being a city slicker, he'd no doubt turn tail and beat it back to Terre Haute when we started bleeding out the first hog. Which was fair enough. Anybody who was husband fodder for a country gal like Tansy would have to stand up to butchering day. I myself wouldn't have put a nickel on Eugene Hammond's chances. So I was pretty sure I knew what Dad was up to.

Before daylight's first streaks, our neighbors came jangling up the lane. Everybody turned out except Tarboxes. Charlie Parr came. His hand rendered him next to useless, but he wouldn't have missed seeing how Eugene Hammond took it when we started lopping the heads off hogs.

Then here came the blazing headlamps of an automobile. Eugene Hammond had taken up Dad's invitation with alacrity, as we said in Spelling School. An automobile at a butchering like to take everybody's mind off business. But we had our way of observing the day, and we stayed faithful to it even in the age of the motorcar.

The water seethed in the barrel, under the tripod where the hogs would hang. The women gathered on the back porch to watch. The barn lot wavered in firelight. Dad had hitched Siren and Stentor to the rock sled, so they'd be ready to drag the carcasses up to the fire.

The three hogs were out of their pen now and in the grove. Dad had his .22 caliber Springfield rifle in hand. Everybody stood by to see who he'd invite to shoot the first one. You never shot your own hogs. You honored a friend with the pleasure of that. Dad handed off the rifle to Mr. Jimmy Leadill, a near neighbor of ours.

Mr. Leadill turned to Eugene Hammond, who wore a mechanic's overalls over his houndstooth suit. I decided right there Mr. Leadill was in on Dad's plan.

He was something of an orator, and said in a carrying voice, "Mr. Hammond, as a welcome stranger among us, you're to have the first shot." He held out the rifle. The other men turned their grins aside. The women gazed from the porch in rare silence.

"But I have to warn you, Mr. Hammond," Mr. Jimmy Leadill went on, "it's one shot per hog. If you don't drop your hog with the first squeeze of the trigger, we can't be responsible for the safety of the neighborhood."

That was a lie, but he told it well.

Eugene Hammond looked surprised to find the rifle in his hands. All Indiana held its breath, and somebody raised a lantern aloft. Quicker than telling it, he shouldered the rifle, sighted down it, and the morning exploded. He'd squeezed off a round and nailed the hog between the eyes.

Blood blossomed from her brow. She sank to her knees, rolling sideways, legs working. Eugene Hammond thrust the rifle back into Mr. Leadill's hands and pulled a pig sticker out of his own polished boot. Before an audience stunned to silence, he strode forth and grabbed a front leg. He inserted the knife into the throat and slashed down to the heart to bleed out the hog in a single move. It kept the blood from clotting the meat.

It was a first-class, professional job. Dad himself couldn't have put down a hog quicker or neater. There hadn't been time for a squeal. Lloyd and Charlie stared. I looked back to the porch to see how Tansy took it. She was just turning back to the kitchen. The neighbors shuffled and cleared their throats. It wouldn't have been polite to show shock.

I was dizzy with amazement. But now it was business as usual, and we all fell to. We hoisted the carcass up on the tripod and fixed the hind legs with the gamble stick. With the block and tackle we worked it up and down in the boiling water. After that, we swung it around, hooked it from the mouth, and dipped the hindquarters. Then we stretched it out to scrape it, and hung it again to rinse it, many hands making light work.

We went right at it, and Charlie did what he could. When it was time to take the head off that first hog, Eugene Hammond somehow had a bigger knife in his hand. Again he stepped forth and in an elegant circular swipe, he sliced around the hog's neck. He dropped the knife, grabbed hold of the ears, and wrenched the head free of the body. Once more quick, neat, and sure. Which I personally thought was close to showing off. Lloyd gaped afresh, and Charlie looked a little hopeless, somehow.

Seemed like Dad's plan to show up Eugene Hammond had backfired on us all. I myself was provoked, but not quite sure why. Didn't I want Tansy off our hands? She was old enough. Our own mother had married Dad when she was seventeen. It would get Tansy out of the teaching trade and off our backs, with any luck before we got to long division. There was naturally a law against a married woman teaching school.

After all, Eugene Hammond wasn't near as ignorant as your typical city person. From his butchering, he'd been a country boy. He gave good presents too. You couldn't fault him there. Thanks to him, we marched into school these mornings to John Philip Sousa strains. We no longer had to start the day with that dumb "We hail our pleasant school" song from Miss Myrt's time.

But handing Tansy off to Eugene Hammond didn't sit right with me. My thoughts were deep but confounded.

After noon dinner in a landscape of steaming innards, coiling sausage, and long pans of scrapple, Eugene Hammond was suddenly before us, drawing on his driving gloves, lowering his goggles.

"How would you fellows like a ride in an automobile, just a spin down as far as the schoolhouse and back?"

"Would I!" Lloyd sang out before I could put a lid on him.

Charlie held out a little longer. But when Eugene Hammond offered to let him crank the automobile with his good hand, Charlie caved in.

Since he'd gone over to the enemy, so to speak, what choice did I have but to follow?

Chapter Fifteen

Fatal Friday

The days grew shorter, along with Tansy's temper. By now, we knew way more than we wanted to. We could tell you the capitals of countries nobody had ever heard of, and their principal exports. Even those of us whose mouths moved when we were reading our own names knew the multiplication table up through times twelve. Seemed like Tansy was looking high and low for any little leftover opening in our heads she could cram knowledge into. And with a heavy hand growing heavier.

Finally, I had a word with Dad. We were down with the pigs one time when I told him Tansy was getting intolerable, one of our Spelling School words. "Dad," I said, "I wish to heaven your plan hadn't blown up in our faces."

"What plan?" Dad was clipping needle teeth on the pigs, so I didn't have his full attention.

"Your plan to show up Eugene Hammond as a tenderfoot at the butchering," I said to refresh his memory.

"Was that my plan?"

"Wasn't it?"

"In fact, it wasn't." Dad gripped a snout. "I invited that young fellow to meet our neighbors in case Tansy was taking to him. It didn't surprise me he was a crack shot. And he mentioned to me himself that he'd come from a rural district over by Gas City, so I supposed he knew his way around a hog."

"Dad," I said, discouraged. "Were you playing fair again?"

"I was trying to," he said. "Son, I've seen you confused before, many a time, but never more than now. If your sister's getting intolerable, why wouldn't you want Eugene Hammond to have her?"

Dad had found the flaw in my argument. I kicked a small hill of pig manure, saying, "Well, why can't she pick Charlie Parr? A fellow would like his sister to marry his best friend, and Charlie's good-hearted. I know he's not broke out with brains. If brains was dynamite, he couldn't blow his nose. But I personally don't think he puts himself forward enough."

Dad pondered. At last he looked up from his task, saying, "I've just thought of a plan, and I think it'll work."

I was all ears.

"Let's let nature take its course."

Glenn Tarbox had helped me put up the school stove. He was still faithful in coming through Aunt Fanny's sugarbush grove every morning, though she'd threatened us all with sudden death if we trespassed. The stove, a front-loader, stayed in the woodshed through warm weather. It weighed about half a ton, but Glenn needed very little help from me to heft it all the way into the schoolhouse.

We set it up by the rostrum on a square of asbestos. We had to hang the stovepipe from the ceiling with strap iron. The pipe rambled across past the mud dauber wasps' nest to a hole in the chimney. Took us two mornings to get it up and fired. Glenn was bringing his noon dinner and his breakfast too in a Karo syrup pail now. I remember one morning he had a right good-looking slab of sour cream apple pie. Though on the quiet side, he was easier company before Charlie got to school.

As for learning and knowledge, I myself thought we were all making pretty fair strides. But did that satisfy Tansy? My head rang around the clock from that cowbell clanging at my spelling.

Then on Thursday morning Mr. George Keating came into the schoolhouse and made right for Tansy with a letter. She went pale and gripped her pointer.

Her knees set her skirts atremble. Silence fell, though somebody whispered, "It's come."

It took its sweet time, because we were into November. The letter was from the County Superintendent of Schools. Now we'd know when Tansy was to be examined and her so-called teaching methods observed. Now we'd learn if Tansy could go on being teacher or if she'd be turned out.

We'd been on the lookout for that letter these many weeks, and waiting hadn't improved Tansy's disposition. It was bound to get here before Thanksgiving. You couldn't count on the roads for a visit from outside after that. The roads around here were nearly impassable.

Mr. Keating hung on to hear the news so he could repeat it. Tansy was all thumbs with the envelope. Finally, Little Britches had to drop down from teacher's chair and come over to help her with it.

Tansy scanned the page while we waited. An icy wind seemed to sweep her, though the stove glowed and you couldn't see your breath even here on the back row.

She looked up and stared sightless across us.

"Tomorrow," she said.

An icy wind swept us all. "Go on," Charlie called from back here, "read out the letter, Tansy."

"Miss Tansy," she said in a broken voice.

Her eyes hurried down the page to the worst paragraph:

I will myself, accompanied by the assistant superintendent, undertake to examine your qualifications as a teacher in an eight-grade rural school with an eye to granting you a provisional teaching certificate.

You will be subjected in the place of your teaching to an oral examination of general knowledge. Your students will demonstrate their acumen and progress during the usual Friday Elocution class.

Horrified silence followed. Then we all squealed once more like pigs under a gate—louder. "Unfair!" we called out. "How come we have to be tested too? We didn't do nothing!"

"This sort of thing never happened under Miss Myrt," Pearl proclaimed. "I personally don't mean to take part and may well be absent. The idea."

She wasn't the only one thinking about being too sick for school tomorrow, though me and Lloyd would never get away with it. If we didn't peel out of bed pretty early, Tansy would touch a match to the mattress.

We were all fixing to riot when she concluded with,

Yours very sincerely for Quality Education,
T. Bernard Whipple,
Parke County Superintendent of Schools.

She was already beginning to recover. In fact, she was laying her plans for tomorrow before Mr. Keating could get on his route with the news.

"This schoolroom needs a thorough cleaning before our . . . company comes. Just look at those windows. And that kindling needs to be in a neat stack. And, Pearl, you'll sweep the floor."

Pearl bridled. "I'll do no such—"

"Pearl, I said you'd sweep the floor," Tansy said, "or I'll sweep it with you." She advanced on Pearl with the pointer and Pearl went for the broom. We all went for something.

On the fatal Friday of Tansy's trial, I was at school with the ladder before sunup. We'd had the stove going for two weeks now, so it was high time to clean out the stovepipe. It was beginning to smoke and seep soot.

I lit a lamp and turned it up. The spit-polished windows shivered in the graying dawn. Not a dead fly decorated the sills. The place was spotless. The Superintendent of Schools could see his face in any surface. The assistant superintendent could eat his dinner off the floor.

Glenn Tarbox stepped up behind me. I jumped a foot.

"Dagnab it, Glenn!" I cried. "You like to scare me out of my skin. What are you doing here so early?"

He was always early. He was trying to keep ahead of Charlie Parr, if you asked me. But this was practically the middle of the night. He had on a starched shirt, blued and ironed flat. His hair had a neat parting, and he'd shaved.

"I don't have that far to come," he said.

"But Stony Lonesome—"

"I don't live out home no more." Glenn looked away. "I live over through the sugarbush at Aunt Fanny Hamline's. She don't keep horses, so I sleep in the tackroom of her barn."

Ha, I thought. What did he take me for? "Glenn, you lying—"

"No, it's the truth. Aunt Fanny put me up when I told her I'd kill my own food, do all her repairs, and run off whoever was stealin' from her."

"But you were the only one stealing from her, Glenn."

"I know it," he said, "but her eyesight ain't up to much."

I stared at him, wondering. "You're not killing all your food, Glenn. You had a nice slab of sour cream apple pie here a while back. Did Aunt Fanny bake it?"

Glenn nodded. "I found her soft spot. Everybody's got one except my maw. I offered Aunt Fanny to work for free."

My head pounded with these disclosures. "And you get along all right with her?"

"Sure," Glenn said, "after I found out where she stockpiled her ammunition and hid it from her."

Still, I couldn't get my mind around it. Glenn Tarbox rooming and boarding with Aunt Fanny Hamline?

"How come, Glenn? Just to be closer to school so you can get ahead of Char—"

"I won't live out home no more," Glenn said. "My brothers were on me day and night about quittin' school. They don't want me gittin' ahead of them. They'd do anything to keep me down."

"Why?"

"That's the way people is who ain't goin' anyplace in life theirselves. They don't want you goin' anyplace either. It was my brothers stuck the puff adder in teacher's desk, and sawed through the board over the ditch. They wanted them crimes pinned on me."

My jaw dropped. This was by far the longest speech anybody'd ever had out of Glenn. I was bewildered. The silence of frosty dawn fell around us. Light began to find the eastern windows.

"We better get them pipes down before Tansy gets here," Glenn said. "How's she doin' this morning?"

"She couldn't keep her breakfast down," I betrayed.

Glenn held the ladder while I went up it. The pipe rose out of the cold stove and angled at the mud daubers' nest. Seemed like the lengths had fitted together easy, but now I couldn't work them loose. Glenn tried, and he couldn't either. The pipes had expanded with the heat, or something.

"Even if we got 'em apart," Glenn said, "the whole business would take the morning."

I could hear Tansy in my head, telling me how I'd left everything to the last minute as usual.

"But they's another way," Glenn said, "quicker." He reached into an overall pocket, behind a belt loop, and drew out a twist of paper. He opened it and showed me a few pinches of gray powder.

"Gunpowder," he said, "about an ounce." Trust Glenn to have an ounce of gunpowder on his person, just in case. "It'll only take that much to clear the stove, pipes, and chimney, all in one puff. Nothin' to it."

With these words, Glenn unlatched the stove door, struck a match to the kindling inside, and threw in the gunpowder.

Then quite a lot happened all at the same time. With an explosion that left my ears ringing well into the new year, the whole stove stood up on its hind legs. The door that Glenn was closing hung loose in his blackened hand. The stovepipe came clattering down from the ceiling, belching a bushel of black soot all over us and the room, including the head of Abraham Lincoln.

Outside, J.W. howled. The backflare from the doorless opening on the stove had singed Glenn and me with a sudden searing. Glenn was solid soot from horns to hoof, though even in his coal-blasted face, you could see his eyebrows were missing. And if his were gone, mine could not be far behind.

"It must of been two ounces," Glenn calculated. The stove door still hung hingeless in his hand. The scene was one of ruin and desolation. Darkness had once more fallen at the soot-blackened windows.

I thought I might have been killed outright by the explosion, but seemed to be standing. Then all of a sudden I'd have been willing to swap this world for a better one because of the voice from behind me. Tansy's.

"Russell Culver, you have ruined my chances as a public school teacher. You meant to and you did. It was your plan from the start."

"No!" I wailed, tasting cinders.

"Gee, Russell," came Lloyd's voice, also from the door, "what did you want to blow the place up for?"

"It wasn't me!" I cried out to heaven. "It was Glenn! He—"

"That's right," Tansy said. "Blame others."

Chapter Sixteen

Two Miracles and a Mercy

By nine o'clock a miracle had taken place. As the pupils got here to find Tansy in what looked like a coal mine, a broken woman, they fell to. Even Pearl scooped a little soot. Little Britches turned back her small sleeves to dust teacher's desk. Charlie wasn't entirely broke up to see Glenn's sorry state, and he put the stove back together. Of course me and Glenn naturally did the work of ten, sweeping, polishing, fitting up the stovepipe: busy as bees, good as gold.

Still, for years after, Tansy swore I'd tried to blow Hominy Ridge School off the face of the earth just to ruin her chances. She was deaf to reason, even when Glenn explained time and again we were only rushing to clean out the stovepipe.

Once the schoolroom looked like its old self, me

and Glenn went out to stick our heads under the pump. Big, scorched shreds of our shirts came away with the soot. Only the bibs on our overalls preserved our modesty.

"I got any eyebrows?" asked Glenn, coming up agasp from the freezing water.

"Not a whisker," I said. "Me?"

"Nothin'," Glenn said. "Over your eyes you're smooth as lard."

Still, we'd all made a miracle. At nine o'clock sharp, Tansy sent Flopears Lumley out to ring the tower bell to begin school, though we were all there. Nobody was out sick. It was way too big a day to miss. When he got as far as the coat room, Flopears yelped with fear and surprise.

"What now?" Tansy murmured. We all turned to see Aunt Fanny Hamline filling up the door frame. She advanced on us in her coal-scuttle bonnet. In one hand her cane, in the other a furled flag.

We shrank.

"State your business," said Tansy, near the end of her rope already.

"Is this a public schoolroom," Aunt Fanny snapped, "or ain't it?"

"It is," we all sighed.

"Is this the day the Superintendent of Schools is coming, or not?"

"It is," we all mumbled.

"Then you need an American flag." Aunt Fanny brandished her flag, and the Stars and Stripes unfurled above us. "This is the same flag my husband, Mr. Hamline, carried into battle at Chicamauga," Aunt Fanny proclaimed. "Three rebel minié balls went through it, but it has stood up right well." She held it high and gave it a shake.

A shaft of sunlight struck through the repolished windows to catch the tattered flag's colors.

Tansy's eyes filled, but she drew herself up and reached for her pointer. "Thank you, Aunt Fanny. It's just what we needed, and it's better than a new one."

Aunt Fanny waved away thanks and turned on her heel. She stumped out, taking a swing with her cane at J.W. as she turned into the morning light.

Charlie put Lester on his shoulder to plant the flag up in its holder. It hung proudly over President Roosevelt and Alton B. Parker.

We were looking good now, like an actual schoolroom. And I knew at last where I stood. She could believe me or believe me not, but what I most wanted in the world was to see Tansy succeed. Why she hankered to be a teacher, I couldn't tell you. But she had chalk dust in her veins, and she deserved to get that certificate. It was only fair.

We heard the jingle of harness outside, and voices.

"On your feet for the Pledge of Allegiance," Tansy

said with a catch in her voice, "quick." Two figures loomed into the schoolroom.

We scrambled up and turned our innocent faces to the flag. Behind us, our visitors had to stand stock-still with their doffed derby hats over their hearts. This slowed them down, but we soon came to "with liberty and justice for all."

"Amen," Flopears said, confusing this with church.

Two men, duded up in town clothes, marched down through us to the rostrum. The one in the lead was a stout party, balder than any egg. He put out a soft pink hand to Tansy, saying, "T. Bernard Whipple, Parke County Superintendent of Schools. This here is my assistant, Mr. Owen."

Mr. Owen had a good head of hair on him and wasn't half as big around as T. Bernard Whipple. He was a young man and altogether a more modern figure, in low shoes. He offered his hand, and Tansy's lingered in it.

We watched.

Mr. Whipple and his assistant superintendent set aside their overcoats and unfolded forms they meant to fill out. Tansy held her ground, a step above them on the rostrum. Her chin was firm, but her eyes were far from certain.

"Without further ado, we will begin," the superintendent boomed, "if you have no objections, Miss Culver."

"None whatever," Tansy said in a faded voice.

"Your age?"

"A lady never gives it," Tansy remarked.

"But a teacher must. How, for example, would we know when you were old enough to draw your pension?"

"Not that it need come to that," Mr. Owen blurted, meaning Tansy might marry and be saved before she was pensioned off. I'll tell you right now, Mr. Owen couldn't take his eyes off her. I wondered if this worked for her or against her.

"Seventeen," Tansy said.

"You are a native-born American citizen?" the superintendent inquired.

"Better than that," Tansy replied with spirit. "I am Hoosier-born and in Parke County." The brooch she inherited from our mother was at her throat to close her collar. It winked in the morning.

The superintendent and his assistant nodded. So far so good.

"And now to your general knowledge."

Us pupils held our breath. How general was her knowledge?

"On the subject of geography, what is the highest elevation in the state of Indiana?"

Search us. Did she know?

Tansy stroked her brooch, recalled, and spoke in a clear voice. "Weed Patch Hill at one thousand one hundred and eighty-six feet above sea level, in Brown County. Known as the Everest of Indiana."

"Excellent!" Mr. Owen said. "Right on the money!"

But the superintendent wasn't so easily pleased. "And now to not waste time, we move right along to the subject of grammar."

We all paled, but Tansy never blinked.

"What is a participle? Does it ever part with its verbal significance? Does it assert action?"

Us pupils hadn't gotten to participles, whatever they might be. Had Tansy?

Yes. She told them all about the participle, though I myself followed little of her reasoning. It was some kind of verb that didn't act like one. Tansy even explained how you better never let your participle dangle.

"Beautifully explained!" Mr. Owen said.

Superintendent Whipple shot him a look of irritation. "Miss Culver," he said, "you will agree that the greatest living poet is—"

"James Whitcomb Riley, now of Indianapolis, the Athens of America," Tansy interjected.

"Quite so. But the first truly Indiana poetic masterpiece is universally considered to be—"

"'The Hoosier's Nest,'" Tansy rapped out, "by John Finley, 1830."

"Miss Culver," Mr. Owen said, "you wouldn't know a line or two of it, would you, by chance?"

Tansy was directing all her answers straight at him now. She cupped her hands and burst into verse:

One side was lined with divers garments,
The other spread with skins of varmints;
Dried pumpkins overhead were strung,
Where venison hams in plenty hung;
Two rifles placed above the door;
Three dogs lay stretched upon the floor—
In short, the domicile was rife
With specimens of Hoosier life.

Mr. Owen caught his breath. "A truly professional rendering, Miss Culver. I have not heard better elocution on the professional stage. Not in Muncie. Miss Culver, not in Fort Wayne."

Tansy blushed slightly and cast down her eyes. I personally thought things were going better than expected. If she could just keep them busy with her answers, maybe they'd never get around to us pupils.

We were all quiet as mice. Ahead of me, Lloyd grew smaller and smaller there between Lester and Flopears.

But after a question or two about arithmetic that went over my head, Mr. Whipple drew a big handkerchief from under his coattails and said, "I think we have heard sufficient from the teacher. But what has she taught?" He gave his nose a big honk, and we all shrank further. Lloyd was practically a dot in the distance.

"It is high time we trained our sights on a few of the pupils." T. Bernard Whipple turned on us. Mr. Owen dragged his eyes off Tansy.

Suddenly, she swept her skirts around him and stepped down from the rostrum, making for Pearl. She reached out and grabbed Pearl's nose between two of her knuckles. Pearl's eyes bugged, and she went an ugly beet-red. But by and by she had to open her mouth to breathe. Then quicker than the eye, Tansy stuck a finger in her mouth and hooked out the chewing gum. She flung the gum in the stove and resumed her stance, straightened her skirts, and folded her hands before her. So they could see she was on top of things, or at least Pearl.

Little Britches cleared her throat noisily. When the superintendent and the assistant had turned on us, they'd turned their backs on her. She didn't like it. They looked back and noticed her for the first time, small in the big chair. Her nose just cleared teacher's desk. Her hair was in sausage curls because this wasn't just any day. She looked up beady-eyed at them.

"Well then, little lady," Mr. Whipple boomed, "what might you be doing sitting in the teacher's place?"

"Heppin' her."

"And I take it this is your first year of school."

"Yep."

"And what is your name?"

"Beulah Bradley," Little Britches said.

"And how old are you?"

"A lady don't—"

"Tell them," Tansy said.

"Six."

"And do you know your letters yet?" T. Bernard Whipple hung over her, big as a house.

"*G* is for the gopher, digging in its burrow," Little Britches remarked. "*H* is for the patient horse, plowing in its furrow."

Beside me, Glenn nodded in agreement. "Ah," said the superintendent. "Can you put the letters together into words?"

Little Britches took up her complimentary writing pad from The Overland Automobile Company and began making big letters with her complimentary pencil. Her tongue escaped the side of her mouth as she labored. At last she held up the pad. It read:

SEE THE FAT MAN

We stirred, but nobody dared break silence. Tansy looked aside. Mr. Owen's jaw trembled. He spoke suddenly. "You are a regular scholar, Beulah. In two or three years you'll be learning your multiplication tables."

"Six eights are forty-eight," Little Britches mentioned.

Mr. Owen stared down at her. "You know your multiplication tables already?"

"Twelve twelves are a hundred and forty-four," Little Britches pointed out.

Mr. Whipple simmered. His ears burned red against his pink head. "Miss Culver, the child is only in first grade. The multiplication tables don't come until—"

"I am here to help her learn," Tansy said, "not to keep her from it. She is the brightest button in the box, and what the others learn, she picks up."

The superintendent jabbed a note on his form with his pencil. He looked out upon us for another victim. We rode low in our desks. *The capital of Missouri is Jefferson City,* I drilled in my head in case I'd get geography. I was wracking my brain for Oregon when the hard Whipple eye fell on me. But it bounced back and forth between me and Charlie and then jumped to Glenn.

Glenn. The superintendent had gone from the youngest of us to the oldest, from the smartest to the—

"Young man, you look of an age to have profited by a good deal of schooling."

Glenn just sat there.

"Come down here and demonstrate what you know."

We all stared at the floor. Tansy too. What schooling Glenn had mastered wasn't going to detain us long. He came out of the desk, long-legged, fully grown. The black rags of his ruined shirt clung to his heavy shoulders. He started down to the superintendent.

But on his way, Glenn swung past the wall and grabbed up teacher's broom. Was he going to sweep out the place? My head swam.

Down front, Glenn swiped at the ceiling with the broom, and the mud daubers' nest broke loose from the rafter and fell into his hands. Stray bits of nest hung in the air and settled on the superintendent's bald dome.

"This here's science," Glenn said, and broke open the nest with his big hands. It fell apart on teacher's desk, and Little Britches peered into it. The mud daubers' nest was untenanted. The wasps had long ago grown and flown. But here was where they'd started out life.

"See these here cells like a comb of honey?" Glenn pointed them out. "The mother mud dauber lays an egg or two in ever' one of them cells. Then she goes to work and stings a spider with her pizen. She don't kill that spider, but she stuns it. Then she sticks that spider in the cell with the egg and shuts it up tight. As the eggs hatch, they've got plenty of spider meat to feed them on. And that's how the mud dauber wasp starts out life."

We were all silenced by this knowledge. It wasn't school-learning from Tansy, of course. All she knew about the life of the mud dauber, she'd just now learned. But Glenn was a country boy. Few of nature's ways were mysteries to him. On the other hand, the superintendent and the assistant were town men. Rockville.

"You learned that at school?" the superintendent inquired.

Glenn shrugged. "Where else?"

"Well, I am glad to see that the study of natural science is not neglected," Mr. Whipple admitted. "But, son, tell me this. Why do you look so surprised? Didn't you know we were coming?"

"I ain't surprised, mister," Glenn replied. "I just don't have no eyebrows." He turned back to his seat, and we all heaved with relief.

That was just before T. Bernard Whipple's gaze fell on Flopears.

I was myself pretty near the end of my rope now. It didn't seem fair. If there was anybody worse to call on than Glenn, it was—

"Boy," Superintendent Whipple barked, "what's your long suit?"

"Who, me?" Flopears pointed to himself. "My what?"

"Come down here and show us what you have mastered. I take it you're not another scholar of the mud dauber."

"Of the what?" Flopears was stumped. He took up his complimentary notepad and wandered down to the rostrum.

Now Flopears, head hung, was there between the superintendent and the assistant. Tansy stood back, pity in her eyes, and dread.

"Well, son, tell us. What are you best at, numbers or letters?"

Flopears tried to think. "Is them my only choices?" He flipped open his notepad on teacher's desk. "I reckon I like pictures best."

The superintendent and the assistant bent over Flopears's notebook. Little Britches too. Mr. Whipple turned to a new page. They all looked closer. Tansy drew nigh.

Then, somehow, we were all on our feet, drifting down to see what was on Flopears's notebook pages.

They were pictures he'd drawn with his complimentary pencil. Pictures like we'd never seen. They ought to have been in frames. There was one of Aunt Fanny in the ditch and all of us trying to heave her out with the bell rope. And you could see it was Aunt Fanny, bigger than a church debt, and all of us. There was the big bow on the back of Pearl's head. And Lester's Buster Brown collar. And me back when I had eyebrows.

Mr. Owen turned a page, and there was a portrait of Tansy, and in one arm Little Britches with her face turned to Tansy's bosom. And in Tansy's other hand the garter snake, coiled with its tail hanging down.

"That's me." Little Britches poked a small finger at the page. "It was the time—"

"That we were studying natural history," Tansy said. "Herpetology."

Flopears had even done a scene of the first day of school, way back in August. We were all racing out of the schoolhouse, J.W. too, barking his fool head off. In the distance the boy's privy blazed like a torch. You could just about smell it.

"Lightning," me and Charlie said together.

You could have knocked us over with feathers. Flopears had captured us all in his notebook. And we were so real, we almost strolled off the page. We'd gotten him wrong. He wasn't a dunce. He was an artist. According to these pages, he saw us all a good deal clearer than we'd ever seen him.

T. Bernard Whipple cleared his throat. "I am glad to know," he said, "that the study of art has not been neglected."

With that, the superintendent and his assistant folded up their forms and reached for their overcoats. It was done with, and there was no doubt in our minds but that Tansy had passed her trial. Another miracle, and a mercy too, since me and Lloyd never had to be called on. So there is some justice in this world, though not a lot.

Chapter Seventeen

Grown and Flown

Of course these events took place years ago, long before your time. It was that year of 1904, when automobiles began to burn up the rural byways. The year airships like boxkites began to darken the skies, though they hadn't found our patch of sky yet. The year my sister, Tansy, got her provisional teaching certificate.

"Well, I hope you're satisfied now," I dared tell her, with the kitchen table between us.

"Far from it," she snapped back. She could snap with very little provocation, as you know. "Has it ever dawned on you that I undertook this entire enterprise to see you through to eighth-grade graduation, Russell Culver? Do you think I didn't know you wanted to wander off to the Dakotas or some outlandish place?

If I didn't turn you around, who would? You have no more direction than a newborn calf, and less judgment. You'll need that eighth-grade graduation certificate to get into Rockville High School."

Had I heard her right? This was at Thanksgiving, so my head still rang like a belfry from the exploding stove.

"High school! Me? How many years would that take?"

"It takes the average pupil four years for a diploma," Tansy calculated. "I'd think you could do it in six."

"And what am I supposed to do with a high school diploma? It is nothing but a durned piece of paper." I oozed outrage.

"You'll need it to get into college," Tansy said. She was very Teacher Tansy now, though we were at home, saved from school by Thanksgiving. "Purdue University, if they'll have you."

"College? And how long would *that* take? Another four years, I suppose."

"At least," Tansy murmured.

"What? You know I'm half deaf."

"I said *at least*."

"I'll be an old man by then," I said. "And *why*, Tansy? I ask you *why*?"

She leaned across the kitchen table at me. Somebody was coming up the back porch steps, maybe Aunt

Maud, so Tansy spoke low and fast. She nearly had me by the throat. "I'll tell you why, Russell Culver. Because it's time you set some kind of example for Lloyd. It's high time you stopped being little brother to me and started being big brother to him. He'd look up to you if there was anything to look up to. And remember this, mister: Everything you can get away with will be Lloyd's burden. Every mistake you make will be his excuse."

And that was it. She turned away, and my fate was sealed. I had to succeed now and do something with my life. What choice did I have?

Tansy was a teacher, make no mistake about it. Down to her toes. She was good and grew better. I'll tell you how good. She not only got me through the eighth-grade graduation exam, she got Charlie Parr through too.

The Board of Education set great store by her. They were even willing to hire a substitute teacher and send her for a winter's course at the normal school in Terre Haute. They forgot she hadn't graduated from high school.

But somehow she never had the time to take off. One winter she was coaching Little Britches for the statewide spelling bee. Another winter she was helping Lester revise his "What Indiana Means to Me" essay for the county contest. It was always something, right up till she married and had to turn in her pointer. By then I was nearly through Rockville High School and looking at the catalog of courses from Purdue.

The twentieth century held some surprises for us all: the flicker of the motion pictures, the yammer of the radio, the mounting rumble of foreign wars, the jangle of change. Aunt Fanny Hamline held out against everything, unto the end. She died at a hundred and three, still hoping to take it all with her.

Dad and Aunt Maud lived long lives too, and felt the setting sun upon their faces. Though Aunt Maud had always maintained she was not long for this world, she outlived all her generation.

At her funeral, the mysterious poet who dwelt among us, the Sweet Singer of Sycamore Township, sang one last song.

When it was time for Aunt Maud's funeral, we of the Methodist church had us a different Reverend Parr, Charlie. You never know who's going to see the light. A pretty fair preacher Charlie turned out to be too, if you ask me. Better than his dad. The poem by the Sweet Singer that Charlie read out at Aunt Maud's funeral went this way:

I seen but little of this world,
Except my corner of it;
The city never drew me,
For I knew I could not love it.
What I loved best was watching

The garden getting ripe
And a pouch of sweet tobacco
And my old cob pipe.

What I loved best was a harvest moon
Before a frosty morn
And lamplight in the barn lot
And them long, straight rows of corn.

I was plain and country;
That's where it starts and ends,
But nobody loved her family more,
Nor treasured more her friends.

I loved the changing seasons,
And looking for life's reasons,
And honey in the comb,
and home.

And so the Sweet Singer sang one final time to us, from the hereafter. For the Sweet Singer had been Aunt Maud herself.

With the educations Tansy made me and Lloyd get, we went out into the world—back east to the great boom of the big city, the topless towers of Indianapolis. There we went to seek our fortunes and find our futures.

Floyd Lumley found his way to Indianapolis too, as

you know from the cartoons he drew for the Indianapolis *Star* newspaper in his famous career. And you'll recall how in the fullness of time Lester Kriegbaum became President of Indiana University and married the Dean of Women.

Both Floyd and Lloyd married Indianapolis wives: strictly city girls who'd gone to Butler University and bobbed their hair.

After we were all married, we went back home to Sycamore Township a good deal, especially in the fall of the year, when that particular world turns gold. We'd get together to laugh and live over the old days when we and the twentieth century were young: Floyd and Lloyd and Lester and their wives, Charlie and Pearl Parr, me and Beulah, Tansy and Glenn.

This book is dedicated to my mother, who entered first grade in a one-room country schoolhouse in the fall of 1912.

And to the memory of my dad, a former country boy dressed in town clothes, when my mother took him home to introduce him to the Leadills and all the country neighbors of my future grandfather, on butchering day.

My dad was a more successful suitor than Eugene Hammond, who vanishes, unchosen, from this story into the urbanity of Terre Haute and the technology of the internal combustion engine.

About the Author

Richard Peck was described by *The Washington Post* as "America's best living author for young adults." He is the first children's writer ever to have been awarded a National Humanities Medal. The author of more than thirty books, he has also won the Margaret A. Edwards Award for lifetime achievement in young-adult literature, the Newbery Medal (for *A Year Down Yonder*), a Newbery Honor (for *A Long Way from Chicago*), and has twice been a finalist for the National Book Award, among countless other honors. He lives in New York City.